STAGES
OF FEAR

Stages of Fear

by

Reggie Oliver

Black Shuck Books
www.BlackShuckBooks.co.uk

Versions of the following stories previously appeared as follows:
'Beside the Shrill Sea' in *Supernatural Tales #5* (2003)
'The Copper Wig' in *The Dreams of Cardinal Vittorini* (The Haunted River, 2003)
'Puss Cat' in *Masques of Satan* (Ash-Tree Press, 2007)
'The Skins' in *Weirdly Supernatural #2* (2004)
'Blind Man's Box' in *Masques of Satan* (Ash-Tree Press, 2007)

Cover design & internal layout © WHITEspace 2020
www.white-space.uk

First published in the UK by Black Shuck Books, 2020

978-1-913038-55-7

*For Jonathan Moore, Actor, Director, Dramatist
and friend of over 40 years*

Like a ballerina's arm, the white sweep of Victorian terraced houses curled gracefully around a sandy bay with high moss-green promontories standing guard over it at either end; a little filigree pier jutted out into the sea; wooded hills and a distant grey castle made up the background. That is how I remember Tudno Bay. The place has a romance about it for me because it was the scene of my professional debut as an actor. I loved Tudno Bay, and even attempted to express my feelings for it in verse, but never really got beyond the first lines which were:

'Beside the shrill sea!
Where learned mermaids sing to me!'

They were an arresting pair of lines, I thought; unfortunately, I could never think of anything as good to follow them, and so they remained, an isolated, fragmentary tribute to the summer of my apprenticeship.

Admittedly the season for which I was engaged at the Grand Theatre, Tudno Bay was not very stimulating artistically. The repertoire consisted of thrillers and comedies, West End cast-offs two decades old; the direction was routine, the company no more than averagely competent. But in those days the sheer joy of acting transcended more pretentious considerations; and the challenge of making something interesting out of uninspired material had its own peculiar excitement. I was never bored because we did a new play every week and never felt overworked because my young memory absorbed words easily.

It was the cloudless summer of 1976 and Tudno Bay was as sun-struck as any Riviera resort. In the mornings we rehearsed; in the afternoons I found some deserted spot where I could spout my lines to the open air, or I would go on expeditions with a fellow performer, Jane, to find props for the show. (Jane and I were the most junior members of the company and were employed as assistant stage managers as well as actors.) In the evenings most of the company would find a bar where we could drink late into the night. Tudno Bay was a respectable place, and the only establishment prepared to accommodate us was Saxon's Bar.

Saxon's was situated in the basement of one of the big Tudno Bay hotels. I was never quite sure whether it was officially a public bar or a drinking club. Whatever it was, nobody seemed to mind its being open at all hours. It consisted of a single, long, low room with a bar at one end. Its decor was nondescript, but the presence of an upright piano and the covering of its walls with framed and signed photographs of minor show business celebrities gave it a certain atmosphere. It was the meeting place for the more raffish element of Tudno Bay society.

We went there initially because one of our company, a middle-aged character actor called Howard, was living with its proprietor, Ray. Howard was a gentle, frog-faced man, one of those modestly gifted, utterly dependable performers destined to be made redundant by the decline of repertory theatre. He had acted in five successive seasons at Tudno Bay during which he had formed a relationship with Ray, and three years previously he had taken up permanent residence at Tudno Bay in Ray's flat.

If it had not been for Howard, we might not have gone so often to Saxon's despite the appeal of its liberal hours. The fact was, none of us liked Ray except Howard, who was besotted by him. Once, perhaps, Ray had been a fine-looking man, but he had long since run to seed. He was in his fifties, tall, heavily built, fat, his features regular but coarsely made. His face seemed to glisten unhealthily from the thin slicked, boot-black hair on his cranium to the rounded red bumps of his aggressively dimpled chin. His small eyes were curtained by folds of shiny pink flesh.

Every evening he was behind the bar at Saxon's drinking, and though his capacity for alcohol was considerable, he regularly exceeded it. Up to a certain point he exuded bonhomie, artificial perhaps and over-effusive but acceptable; then one drink would tip the scale: the mask slipped and the creature behind it was revealed.

One sensed rather than consciously recognised the moment when this change took place because it was only towards the very end of a night's session that he became overtly aggressive. He might begin by retailing some outrageously malicious tale about a local Tudno Bay worthy. Had we heard that the Headmistress of Tudno High was having an affair with two of her sixth-formers, or that the Mayor had exposed himself to a young boy in the Pier toilets? He would then invite one's reaction to this piece of news. If it was muted Ray would accuse you of prudishness; incredulity was seen as tantamount to calling him a liar; a flippant approach was heartless and shallow. There must have been a way of reacting to him which would have defeated his desire to create tension and anguish, but I never discovered it. Ray had a subtlety of technique in such matters which his appearance belied.

But this was not the worst of it: when he turned his attention to Howard he was a demon. There was, it is true, some scope for his mockery. Howard cultivated certain eccentricities of dress which might have seemed odd even on someone less ungainly than him. He wore suits which were too tight for him and quite out of style. He believed in every kind of psychic nonsense and attended a Spiritualist church in the town. His good-natured credulity was such that he would believe almost anything one told him. Ray took full advantage of all these and other weaknesses, so skilfully sometimes that you laughed, only to feel guilty about it afterwards. If you protested, Ray would say he was only having a bit of fun, what business was it of yours? Anyway, old Howie didn't mind, did he? Howard, who clearly did mind, would put on a ghastly pretence of enjoying it all. Perhaps he knew that if he didn't pretend Ray would make it hell for him when they were alone.

Many times Jane and I would agonise over whether we should go to Saxon's after the show. We often decided we should not, but then Howard would beg us to come. Perhaps he derived some relief from having his humiliations witnessed by sympathetic friends. I hope so, but the memory of those times is still painful to me. Once Jane, who was bolder and more direct than I was, asked Howard why he put up with Ray. Howard said: 'Oh, I know, he can be a bit of a – well, I don't like to use the word, but a bit of a so-and-so sometimes. But when we're in the flat he can be quite different.'

'The Flat', as he invariably called it, featured largely in Howard's conversation. Every lunch time, however inconvenient it was, he had to get back from rehearsals to the flat to make Ray's lunch. He would tell us if he had been cleaning the flat, or if some minor improvement, always suggested by Ray, had been made to its appointments. If one of the company jokingly asked how the flat was that day, Howard would answer the question gravely, as if 'the flat' were an ailing elderly relative. Some of us once expressed a great desire to see the flat, but Howard mumbled something about Ray and turned our request aside. Evidently Ray had put the place out of bounds to anyone not directly sanctioned by him.

Our season was long: it began in May and ended in October. Towards the end of June we noticed that Ray's behaviour was worsening appreciably. After one night at Saxon's when Ray had reduced Howard to tears, Jane and I decided not to set foot inside the bar again. The following morning at rehearsals Howard took it upon himself to apologise to us for Ray.

'It's the drink,' he said. 'I try to tell him to keep it moderate, but he won't. The doctor said he had six months to live if he went on like this. He said the doctors are always saying you've got six months. And he won't listen to me. He says I'm an old woman. I think Trevor encourages him.'

Trevor, or "Trev" as Ray called him, was a new figure on the scene and another reason why we no longer visited Saxon's. Ray had picked him up somewhere and he had become part of the ménage at the flat. He was barely out of his teens with lank black hair and a white face that had seen more than it should have at his age. He dressed in black leather and barely spoke a word. At Saxon's he would stand behind the bar with Ray and occasionally whisper in his ear. Jane, in particular, found his presence troubling; and it was true that since his arrival Ray's teasing of Howard had become even more poisonous.

The month of July had almost passed before the company experienced a sequence of events which changed our lives. For Jane and myself these happenings had a prelude which may or may not have a bearing on the story.

It was Sunday evening, our one night off of the week, and Jane and I were walking along the front. We had vague plans of going to a concert at the Pier Pavilion, the weather was fine and we were full of youthful well-being. Suddenly Jane stopped. Turning to look at her I had the curious experience of seeing the colour quite literally vanish from her face within a matter of seconds. Before my eyes she turned from a robust twenty-four-year-old to a frightened girl of sixteen. When I asked what the matter was she shuddered and said that a man – or something – in black had just walked through her. Jane often had psychic moments like this about which I was puzzled but not resolutely sceptical, because her approach to them was too matter of fact to excite scorn. The experience so disturbed her that she said she no longer felt like going to the concert.

We turned back towards our digs. The sun was beginning to lower itself into the sea behind a raft of dusky pink cloud. Few people were about, as this was the time in the evening when the holidaymakers were eating their tea. We could see their pink faces bent over the sauce bottles in the windows of small hotels and boarding houses all along the front. The tide was in and the shore almost deserted. A few hundred yards away from us a solitary male figure was hurling stones violently into the sea. Some trick of the light, or perhaps our troubled imaginations, made the figure, dressed all in black, seem unnaturally tall and thin. As we came closer we could hear that he was singing to himself, some kind of unidentifiable rock tune in a high sexless whine. As the song reached a crescendo he threw a stone high into the air. We watched as the stone described its arc then dropped with barely a splash into the dark sea. For a moment the whining stopped; then it began again.

'My God, that's Trevor,' said Jane. 'Let's get out of here.'

The following morning, I arrived at the theatre for rehearsal to find that Howard was not there. This was unusual because, though I was early, Howard was invariably earlier. There he would be, sitting in the Green Room sipping a coffee and studying his stars in the *Daily Mirror*. As the rest of the company trickled in each of them asked jocularly what had happened to Howard? They missed him. They needed him to read out their stars as he always did. But he did not come, and our director, Len was also late.

When Len did arrive, he had on his serious face: 'Boys and girls, I had a telephone call this morning. Yesterday evening our friend Ray had a stroke. Apparently, he'd been drinking all day. He was rushed to hospital but he got worse. He died last night. As you can imagine Howard is pretty distressed about it all. I have let him off this morning's rehearsal, so we'll just have to work round him, but he's coming down to do the show in the evening. I think that is for the best. Howard is a professional. The show must go on.'

Len's philosophy of life was based entirely on such tired theatrical clichés. His religion was 'professionalism'. 'I may not be the most brilliant, innovative director in the world,' he used to say, 'but I am a professional, and I could teach some of these arty farty types a thing or two about theatre.' Jane and I liked to imagine those mythical 'arty farty types' sitting at his feet, imbibing his advice on how to make an entrance through a French window.

That morning Len rehearsed all the scenes in which Howard did not appear with the air of someone who had been dealt a grave personal injury but was bearing up manfully under the strain. At about midday, much to everyone's discomfort, Howard put in an appearance, saying that he wanted to rehearse. Everyone gathered round to console him and, as a result, rehearsals were abandoned.

Howard sat in the Green Room, sipping coffee and recalling Ray's last hours in minute and repetitive detail: how he had started drinking early that day and would not listen to Howard's call for moderation; how the stroke had happened and Howard had called the ambulance; how before Ray finally lost consciousness his last word was the faint utterance of Howard's name. To our embarrassment Howard gave us an impression of Ray's last words: 'How... ard... How...ard... Like that,' he said. It turned out that Ray had drifted into death at about the time when Jane had her uncanny experience.

'Where was Trevor during all this?' she asked. For the first time Howard, who had been telling his story in a numbed monotone, became animated.

'Well, when Ray had his stroke, Trevor just sat there in the flat. He didn't do anything. He looked at Ray, sort of laughing, and he said: "Told you so." Just that. Then I telephoned the ambulance, and when it came he was gone. I got back to the flat – oh, I don't know – sometime this morning, and he'd been and taken things.' The last two words, sobbed out, opened the floodgates of grief and Howard wept in Jane's arms.

The rest of us became indignant about Trevor. What had he taken? Apparently the missing items included some small pieces of antique silver and the gold bracelet with *Ray* engraved on it which Howard had given his dead lover. We must phone the police, we said, but Howard had lapsed again into indifference and said they would never catch him. Nonsense, we said, who was this Trevor? Where did he come from? Howard had no idea. He didn't even know his surname. He was just Trevor.

That night Howard gave a word perfect and acceptable performance as the police inspector in *Murder Must Out*. We were all relieved and Len, who had been disgruntled all day, seemed mollified. He offered Howard's conduct to Jane and me as an instance of 'what professionalism is all about.'

Howard never broke down or failed to perform adequately on stage; he merely settled into a state of inert gloom, and his misery was compounded by a number of unpleasant shocks.

As he repeatedly insisted to us, he had never expected anything from Ray's will, but to be left nothing except Ray's portrait in oils was obviously a disappointment. Other more substantial bequests were made to various friends in the town, and the bulk of Ray's fortune, including the lease on Saxon's and the flat, was left to Ray's son, Terry. Howard, like the rest of us, had known nothing of Terry's existence, but he was soon to be made painfully aware of it when Terry and his wife arrived for the funeral. They treated Howard as a miscellaneous nuisance and he was blamed for the theft of the silver which apparently 'belonged to the family.' He was given twenty-four hours in which to vacate the flat.

At the height of the holiday season it was hard to find somewhere to stay, but a number of unexpected people, indignant about his treatment, offered Howard a room in their houses. He refused them all. Howard felt he needed solitude rather than sympathy, so, with his few possessions and the portrait in oils of Ray, he took up residence in one of the unused dressing rooms of the Grand Theatre, sleeping on a mattress on the floor.

This was strictly speaking not allowed, but the management of the company was based in London and Len, who was its representative, did not have the heart to forbid him the theatre. Though none of us admitted as much, we all found Howard's decision to sleep at the Grand disquieting. A theatre is a place to visit and perform in; to live there is to inhabit a limbo. We would happily talk to him on the stairs or in the Green Room, but we avoided visiting him in his dressing room. One of the causes of our reluctance was the portrait.

It was a three-quarter length of Ray as a young man at the zenith of his coarse good looks. There was a slight smile on his parted lips and a vacancy in the blue eyes which seemed to look out of the canvas, over the shoulder of a viewer, like a social climber at a cocktail party. With its gaudy flesh tones, confident brush strokes and bright blue background the painting was clearly the work of a journeyman artist of some accomplishment and no talent. Yet, for all its slick vacuity, the painting held one's reluctant attention, perhaps because the manner of its execution so clearly complemented the nature of its subject. In its elaborate gilded frame it hung on the wall of Howard's dressing room, presiding over his few sombre possessions.

'He was the love of my life and I'll never see him again,' said Howard when he first showed me the picture. I tried hard to keep my prejudices in abeyance, but I found Ray's domination over Howard's thoughts even more repulsive in death than it was in life. Howard seemed to make no effort to work through his grief; he was held in suspension. His conversation, never lively at the best of times, trod the same dreadful circle of mourning and memory day after day. It was inevitable perhaps that some clairvoyant at his spiritualist church would vouchsafe him the information that Ray had passed safely over and was 'watching over him'. Howard repeated this phrase to us with melancholy satisfaction, but we thought of the picture and shuddered.

Some weeks went by during which I became used to Howard's peculiar way of life and stopped worrying about it. I was young and the sun shone. The adventure of acting engrossed me and his tragedy became little more than the sombre shade which threw the hopeful colours of my existence into greater relief.

Towards the end of July I began to notice that there was sometimes alcohol on Howard's breath when I was on stage with him. This was disturbing in someone whose avowed rule was never to take a drink before a show, but, as his performance did not seem to suffer, I took little notice. One evening I came into the theatre early and heard voices coming from Howard's dressing room which was the one nearest the stage door entrance. One of the voices was Howard's, the other – unintelligible – was a hissing whisper. I thought Howard might have been going through his lines, but the words he spoke were not from any play. Interspersed with the strange indecipherable whisper they were:

'No... No, don't... No, don't say that... No don't...'

Feeling acutely embarrassed I turned back and shut the stage door loudly, coughing as I did so, to make Howard believe that I had just come in. The voice and the whisper stopped abruptly. Howard came out of his dressing room and asked me how I was. He did not seem unduly agitated, just a little dazed. Peering through his open door I noticed that the taps of his dressing room basin were on. The pipes hissed, and I reassured myself that this was the whispering I had heard.

~

My digs were not far from the theatre. I occupied a single roomed 'holiday flatlet' on the top floor of a block of similar rooms. My window looked down the street towards the Grand Theatre. One hot, airless night in early August it was open. I went to sleep to the familiar sounds of desultory traffic and the occasional late reveller; then at about two in the morning I awoke suddenly. I thought I had heard a cry of alarm, though it was hard to say of what kind because I had woken out of a tangle of dreams.

I went to the window and looked out. The street was deserted; no voices were to be heard, but there was something unnatural about what I saw. It was the light. There seemed to be a glow where there should not have been. I looked further out of the window and smelt something acrid on the night air. I could just see one of the windows of the theatre brightly lit from the inside by a yellow flickering light. Slowly my waking mind gathered these impressions together and formed a conclusion. The Grand Theatre was on fire.

I ran down three flights of stairs and had just got to the pay phone in the hall when I heard the ring of fire engine bells sweeping down the road to the theatre. Howard was inside the building and I knew where he was. The next moment I was running down the road towards the fire.

The hours that followed are a confused memory. I have no idea what I did most of the time but I know that it was seven o'clock and the sun was well up when someone drove me back to my digs from the hospital, still wearing pyjamas and dressing gown. It all seems more of a dream to me as I remember it, because, as in a dream, I was helpless and inappropriately dressed.

I remember the black acrid smoke billowing out of a first-floor dressing room window, the steam and spray of the hoses. I remember shouting in a fireman's ear for what seemed like minutes, trying to make him understand that there was someone in the building, the long agonising moments before Howard's unconscious body was dragged out, the ride to the hospital, attempts to resuscitate him and their failure. Even now it is only my reason which can place these events in their true sequence.

When the dawn came the theatre was a blackened smoking shell and Howard was dead. His presence in the theatre that night caused infinite trouble. The insurance company refused to pay up because he was there illegally and must have caused the fire. The Tudno Bay Council who owned the theatre sued the management of our theatre company, and the management contemplated suing us. As it happened no-one paid up because the cause of the fire was never definitively established. All that was certain was that it had not begun in Howard's dressing room. He had died of suffocation from the smoke fumes.

A few days after the fire the company dispersed. Jane and I alone stayed on to go to Howard's funeral. It was a deeply melancholy affair because, beside an elderly aunt who had travelled over from Liverpool, Howard appeared to have no close relatives and Jane and I were the only friends present. The only other person to attend the cremation was one of the firemen. After the service he came over to speak to me. It was clear that something was on his mind. After some moments of inconsequential talk, I asked if he was the one who had carried Howard out of the burning building.

'No,' said the fireman, 'I was there, but that was Dafydd. He can't be here. Off sick. Funny thing, you know. Dafydd's a good man, a strong man: not much upsets him, but that fire did. It was something he saw when he was getting your man out. There was a lot of smoke, as you know, and the things in his room were what we call smoke damaged. You know what I mean? Everything is covered with this thin layer of soot. You can never get the smell out of clothes when they've been smoke damaged. Terrible. But Dafydd could see that there was one thing in that room that was not smoke damaged at all, and he couldn't find no explanation, see. It's upset him no end, and I can't quite see why. But it is what you might call – well – odd, you might say.'

When I asked him what item it was that had escaped the smoke damage I had already guessed, but I wanted to be wrong.

'It was this painting. Portrait it was. Good piece of art, I'd say. A young man kind of smiling. Handsome face, not nice though.

Forensics have it and they can't explain no smoke damage either. Another funny thing. Your man, he'd not died asleep. He'd woken up and tried to get out. Now it's natural for people to get confused in smoke-filled rooms, but he'd found the door all right. There was blood on the handle and his hands were all bloody too. But why didn't he manage to get out? His door was never locked or anything.'

The fireman paused and looked into the distance at nothing in particular. I sensed that he had more to tell.

"You know, there was this old lady who lived over the road. She was the one who rang the fire brigade. She swears she heard voices coming from that building. From two people, not just the one. One was frantic, screaming like, but there was another, sort of slow, a bit drunk like, laughing almost. She said that voice fair gave her the horrors, much more even than the screaming which was bad enough."

"Did she hear what the voice was saying?"

"Nothing much. Just 'How…ard! How…ard! How…ard!' Like that. Fair gave me a fright even to hear her saying it. Wasn't that the name of your friend who died?"

We could not reply. When the fireman had left us Jane and I walked for a while in the dreary crematorium garden without speaking.

'Well, at least he's free of Ray now,' I said eventually.

'Not unless he wants to be,' said Jane.

A monologue for an actor

The year is 1930 and Mr F. Harrison Budd, an actor in his sixties, with a fine head of hair, appears to be giving a lecture to a large, attentive audience.

Good evening, ladies and gentlemen. How pleasant to see so many good people here. And welcome to my lecture entitled "Random Reminiscences of a Strolling Player by F. Harrison Budd..." That's me... My name is F. Harrison Budd, actor, late of the Theatre Royal Drury Lane, His Majesty's Theatre, the Lyceum etcetera etcetera. Oh, yes. I've acted with them all. Forbes Robertson, Alexander, Tree... *(imitating the actor Tree, a Jewish voice)* "The roof of your mouth is like the dome of St Pauls..." Tree as Svengali in *Trilby*, you know. Magnificent performance. Mag-nificent. Then there was Irving... (*imitating the actor Irving*)

Now is the winter of our discontent
made glarious sammer by this san of Yark...

San of Yark... Strange, but curiously effective... However to proceed... Random Reminiscences of a Strolling Player... Yes... I was born in the year 1872, the son of Ezekiel Harrison Budd, a corn merchant in the city of Manchester. My father made every effort to interest me in the useful trade of... er... merchandising corn, but 'twas of no avail. From an early age I was destined for the stage. I remember... I recall... What? I remember... But you don't want to hear all this do you? I know what you want... You want to hear the story of the Copper Wig. Very well... This once... This one last time.

It was in the early summer of 1893 – I think – yes. 1893 that I was summoned to join Mr. Alfred Manville's theatrical company at the town of Yarborough in the North of England. I would have preferred to wait for a London engagement

– Tree had promised me something in his next season, you know. Yes – but well youth, youth! My finances were perilously low, my landlady and tailor exigent... Besides, Manville had a fair reputation. Used to be known as "the Macready of the North", you know. But when I knew him he was content to manage the company, play the character roles and leave the leading parts to younger men.

Our tour of the Northern Circuit was to open with I think *One of the Best* and *Harbour Lights*, dramas made popular at the Adelphi Theatre by the ill-fated Mr. William Terriss. You remember. Murdered by a mad actor at his own stage door. But that is by the by... I was engaged for a number of minor but not wholly negligible roles The company was a comparatively small one, no more than a dozen or so players, but Manville, we used to call him "the Guv'nor", he used to put on a pretty lavish show simply by employing "supers" in every town we visited. Supers? Amateurs. Did it for free. Very enthusiastic. They would play very small parts, populate the crowd scenes, get in our way, that sort of thing. Often supplying their own costumes too. All they asked in return was a pint or two of good ale after the show with us professionals and the privilege of boasting that they had once appeared in Mr Manville's company.

Now the Guv'nor – perhaps for safety's sake, perhaps on the principle of "divide and rule" – had engaged two leading men, Mr. Edwin Marden and Mr. Charles Warrington Fisher. Two leading men. What a contrast in character and talents! Mr Fisher was the subtler performer. Marden on the other hand was dashing and undoubtedly the favourite with the public, largely perhaps because of his looks. But Fisher was by no means bad looking... However, Marden was half a head taller than him, wiry and muscular in build, strikingly handsome. What perhaps distinguished them most, and advantaged Marden, was in the matter of hair. Fisher's hair was pale, fine and, to tell an unvarnished truth, receding, but Marden had a magnificent head of wavy, copper-coloured locks. Fisher often resorted to a wig. Wigs are all very well, they can never compete with the genuine article. Audiences in those days could be very cruel on actors they detected wearing them. Picture a tender scene of romance. Suddenly a voice cries out from the gallery: "Remove your headpiece, sir, in front of a lady!"

Well... Contrary to what one might expect, Marden and Fisher were not rivals in the normal sense of the word. They did not quarrel or divide the company into warring factions. Very polite to each other... They even used to share lodgings, but under the surface they were very different beings. Marden: breezy, outgoing and addicted to long walks when he had the leisure; Fisher: more thoughtful and inward looking. If he took a walk it was to investigate sixpenny bookstalls in the town, or study the architecture of the local church.

Our first weeks were harmonious and successful. Marden and Fisher had equal status and billing in our first two plays, but I was conscious of a certain atmosphere developing between them when the Guv'nor decided to put into the repertoire that fine drama *The Honour of the Tremaines.* This ever popular play was to be his chief attraction, and he decided to cast Marden in the leading role with Fisher supporting him as the hero's friend.

The play is in four acts, but the great moment comes at the end of the third. You are all familiar of course with *The Honour of the Tremaines?* No? Oh dear. Well, in that case I must, for purposes which will become evident, briefly summarise the plot. Apart from the first act, the scene is laid in India where Roger Tremaine and his friend Hubert La Rose are officers in the Loamshire Regiment at Bangrapore. Now Tremaine, you see, has come to India under a cloud, having in the first act taken the blame for an incident of cheating at the card table of which Roger Tremaine's elder brother, the Marquess of Tremaine was actually guilty. Tremaine takes the guilt upon himself in order to protect the Honour of the Tremaines and save the title from disgrace. In India he becomes popular with the regiment and falls in love with Emily, the Colonel's daughter. Sweet girl. Played by the Guv'nor's daughter, Miss Rose Manville. Unfortunately there is a rival for her heart in the shape of one Captain Frederick Vosper. Vosper, the villain of the piece. He contrives that Tremaine should fall into the hands of Nazir Ali, a ferocious local bandit. So all is set for the great third act, the final scene of which is laid in the officer's mess of the Loamshires at Bangrapore. Picture it. Candle light. Splendid scarlet uniforms. A practical meal, supplied by the guv'nor. Conversation at dinner turns to the incident which drove Tremaine from England at which point Captain Vosper says:" I say Tremaine is a blackguard!" Incensed by this, Tremaine's friend Hubert La Rose rises from the table and thunders: "To any man who says that Roger Tremaine is a blackguard I give the lie!" Tremendous applause. But this fine moment is eclipsed by what follows, for through the double doors of the mess staggers a man in the tattered uniform of an officer of the Loamshires. It is Tremaine himself who has escaped from the clutches of Nazir Ali! "I give the lie myself!" he cries and collapses onto the table. Tumultuous applause. Curtain. Terrific moment. Never failed. Except... Well, I'll come to that.

Now, when I tell you that it was Fisher who played his faithful friend Hubert La Rose – "To any man who says that Roger Tremaine is a blackguard I give the lie!" – but it was Marden who took the role of Tremaine – "I give the lie myself!" Well, you can imagine – quite a difference – what a gulf was fixed between them in the eyes of the public. For that part alone Marden became "the idol of the ladies and the envy of the men."

I have to say that Marden took full advantage of the benefits conferred by the role. His success with the ladies of each town he visited was remarkable, a success he took with an easy careless arrogance which was not altogether likeable. He began to put on airs.

It was in Doncaster that there occurred an incident which significantly worsened relations between Fisher and Marden. They had taken lodgings together at a Mrs Pardoe's. Mrs Pardoe had a daughter named Judith, I think, yes, Judith, a beautiful girl of nineteen. Fisher was greatly attracted. Indeed, I believe that he had formed an attachment to her during a previous stay in the town and they had corresponded. However, the long and the short of it was that in the course of the week Marden managed to erm – well, not to put too fine a point on it... er... seduce the young lady and, worse still, boasted of the conquest to some of his cronies in the company. When they pointed out to him that his friend Fisher had an interest in that direction he winked. "Ah, you see," he said, pointing meaningfully to his magnificent locks, "I won that race by a head." It was accounted a great witticism in the company and was oft repeated. Not surprisingly when Fisher came to hear of it he was enraged. He said little at the time, but when Marden approached him at the end of the week and suggested they share lodgings once again, Fisher turned on his heel and stalked away from him in silence.

Relations between the two in the ensuing weeks got so that they barely spoke a word except on stage. The frost was greatly exacerbated by the extraordinary success of *The Honour of the Tremaines*. The Guv'nor dropped the other plays in his repertoire, and Marden's personal triumph was reflected in the billing. His name now appeared above the title and in letters twice as large as anyone else's (except, of course, the Guv'nor's).

However, by the time we reached Slowbridge Fisher and Marden seemed to be on better terms. Do you know Slowbridge, that drab and deleterious Midlands town? No? Your state is the more blessed. For the first time in many weeks they exchanged cordial greetings in the theatre. It would seem that Fisher had become reconciled to playing second fiddle, though, in the light of what happened next, I have my doubts.

It was on the Thursday evening of the Slowbridge week. I was making up in a dressing room of the Regent Theatre with several of my fellow performers, when the call boy knocked to give us the quarter, twenty minutes before curtain up. Unusually for him, having knocked he entered and announced to us that Mr Marden was not in his dressing room, had not come into the theatre at all. We said that he should tell Mr. Manville, but the boy seemed fearful. Well, he realised that he should have alerted the management when Marden had not arrived at the half. I agreed to go with the boy to beard the Guv'nor in his lair. When Manville heard the news:

"Hold the curtain for no longer than five minutes in case Marden turns up. Mr Fisher should prepare to take over the role of Tremaine, you, Mr Budd, are to attempt the part of the hero's friend, Hubert La Rose. Do you know the lines?"

"Yes, Guv'nor. I think so!"

"Think so!"

"Yes, Guv'nor. I do."

"Very well then. Mr Willington, our junior character man, will double your part, the role of Lieutenant Beauhampton, with that of his own, the comic Indian servant Babu. Now, about your business straight!"

So it was. Marden failed to appear and we all went on and – perhaps out of sheer terror of the Guv'nor – we were word perfect in our altered parts.

But Marden had disappeared without a trace. His movements on that day, as far as could be ascertained by the Police, were as follows. The morning had been spent at his lodgings in Wendell Street. At noon he had ventured out for a walk and met Mr Fisher outside the White Hart Hotel in the centre of town and there they had luncheon together. Witnesses declared that the two men had appeared to be on the most convivial terms. At two o'clock they left the White Hart together and then, according to Fisher, had gone their separate ways: Marden to walk by the canal, Fisher to examine the famous misericords in the choir stalls of Slowbridge church. After that there had been only one doubtful sighting of Marden. He had been seen by an itinerant match seller from the other side of the canal running along the towpath, apparently in a state of some agitation. When asked if anyone been following Marden the witness replied that he could not be sure.

Naturally some suspicion fell on Fisher, but no evidence could be found to contradict his account of events. Moreover, there was no body and so no certainty that there had been any foul play. Marden's disappearance cast a shadow over the company, but the great principle of "the show must go on" prevailed. Only one member of the company was inconsolable and this was our leading lady Miss Rose Manville, the Guv'nor's daughter, with whom, it would appear, Marden had "an understanding".

Fisher took the role of Tremaine very well indeed and if he was not quite as dashing as Marden he was perhaps more soulful, especially in the scenes with Miss Manville. (Miss Manville, however, had a great aversion to Fisher though, trouper that she was, she never showed it on stage.) Fisher's wig, it was true, was not wholly satisfactory and often provoked a few derisive titters on his first entrance, but even this problem was solved, as I shall tell.

Three weeks after Marden's disappearance we were playing at the – I think, yes – the Alhambra Theatre, Derby (now alas a cinematograph palace). On our first night there Fisher sent a note by the call boy summoning me to his dressing room. Fisher had befriended me and I had responded after a fashion. We had similar, bookish tastes, but there was always something remote about him that I could never get behind. Closeness was barred and companionship taken up and dropped very much at his whim.

That night, as I entered his dressing room, Fisher seemed to be in a state of high excitement. A square cardboard box with a printed label on the top was situated in the middle of his dressing table. His eyes glittered and he wore a gleeful smile which did not seem to me entirely pleasant. He beckoned me over...

"What do you think this is? It came by carrier today!"

Obviously baffled astonishment was called for. I duly obliged.

Like a conjurer performing an important trick, he removed the lid of the box with a flourish and from a nest of tissue paper out came a magnificent copper coloured wig. Then, with another flourish, he placed the wig on his head. It was astonishing. Even without the gauze stuck down with spirit gum the hair looked as if it belonged to him. It was a triumph of the wigmaker's art. I congratulated him. He beamed exultantly. Once again I was conscious of something not quite nice about all this elation. I searched for a reason for my unease, and then it suddenly occurred to me: the hair was identical in colour and consistency to *(shout)* Marden's! For a moment my horror must have become apparent because he looked at me enquiringly.

I asked him: "Are you going to wear that tonight?"

"Yes. Of course. Why not?"

"Well, if I were you, I'd show it to Miss Manville first, before you go on stage with her."

"Why?"

"I am amazed that you should ask. You are surely aware of the theatrical etiquette which stipulates that if an actor is going to wear something radically different from his normal garb on stage, he should go round the dressing rooms and inform his fellow performers beforehand."

I did not mention the name of Marden. It would have stuck to my lips.

At this Fisher merely nodded, patted me on the back and went off in the direction of Miss Manville's dressing room.

About half a minute later I was standing in the backstage corridor when I heard a woman scream. I arrived outside Miss Manville's dressing room to find her being revived by her dresser with smelling salts. She had been having hysterics but by the time the curtain went up she had recovered and, like the trouper she was, gave the usual admirable performance. However, she never again spoke a single word to Mr Fisher other than on stage.

Something else of note happened at Derby. Towards the end of the week news reached us that the body of a man had been found floating in a backwater of the Slowbridge Canal. There were signs that the body had been weighted down with stones, but that these weights had come loose and the corpse had floated to the surface. No watch or pocket book was found on the body to identify him, but the clothes were similar to the ones Marden had been wearing on the day he disappeared. Certain identification was impossible because of one dreadful fact: the head was missing. Indeed, despite extensive draggings of the canal and other searches, it was never found.

Our next few weeks were the most successful so far of the tour. The wig seemed to give Fisher a confidence he had never known before so that he managed to combine his own subtlety with some of Marden's dash. He became a firm favourite with the public, but off stage he remained his old subdued and introspective self.

One oddity about him that I noticed was that he would never let the wig out of his sight. Once the performance was over he would place the wig on its block, into the cardboard box and take it back to his lodgings. Sometimes he would actually wear it during the day. One morning I saw him from the back walking down Acker Street in Manchester. For a moment I could have sworn it was Marden. When I asked him who had made this wonderful wig for him he gave an evasive reply, and on looking for the label on the top of the cardboard box I noticed that it had been carefully removed.

I also began to notice something strange

happening during the performance. There were moments when it seemed to me that Fisher's lines were spoken by two people at once. This was particularly the case during the third act which I have described. There were nights when that great curtain line "I give the lie myself!" seemed to have an odd echo in the theatre, an echo which did not quite correspond with Fisher's intonation of the line. "I give the lie myself!... I give the lie myself!... I give the lie myself!" On one of these occasions I saw that Fisher too had noticed the echo. A split second before he crashed dramatically onto the mess table a terrible look of fear and rage passed across his face.

Fisher started to have an aversion to being alone and, when we reached Castleford, he asked me to rent with him what is known in theatrical parlance as a "combined chatsby", a sitting room with two adjoining bedrooms. I was reluctant, but he seemed very anxious that I should join him, and his gratitude when I agreed was effusive and, frankly, rather pathetic. In those days you know the landladies used to come to meet the theatrical Sunday trains to tout for custom on the platform. Fisher spent some time haggling with a number of these women before deciding on one of them.

So we settled in to our digs late that morning and the landlady served us a passable Sunday dinner in our shared sitting room. After dinner Fisher insisted I go out with him on a walk, so we went out to tramp dully about the town. Though he seemed to need me to be with him, he was not much of a companion: he talked in grunts and monosyllables. He led the way but in no particular direction as if bent only on filling the time strenuously between dinner and tea. I noticed also, rather to my relief, that he had given up wearing the wig during the day, settling for a grey bowler alone to cover his baldness.

By the time we had returned from our walk I was exhausted, but Fisher was still imbued with nervous energy. On entering the sitting room, Fisher, ahead of me, stopped suddenly, said:

"What did you do that for?"

I thought he must mean me. I said, "Eh?"

He started, as if he had forgotten I was there. Then he pointed to the mantelpiece on which stood the copper wig on its wig block. It had its back to us, and it occurred to me that the thing could have been mistaken for a severed head.

He asked me "Did you put that there?"

But I knew that he knew that I hadn't. He did not wait for my denial but immediately went to the fireplace, snatched the wig off the mantelpiece and took it into his room. I was reminded irresistibly of a mother carrying a fractious child off to bed. From the bedroom I could hear what sounded like muttered scoldings. Fortunately at this moment our landlady came in with the tea. I began to wish devoutly that I had never accepted his offer of a combined chatsby.

My bedroom looked onto the street and on my first morning there I remember being woken before dawn by the clatter of clogs on cobbles as the mill workers went to the factory. It did not disturb me; in fact it gave me the selfish pleasure of knowing that I could turn over deliciously in bed and not think about work until the evening. I was warm and drowsy, safe in the knowledge that I would soon be asleep again, but something was preventing me. In my half-woken state it took me some time to identify the disturbance. It was voices, one clear, the other muffled, which seemed to come from the sitting room, or from Fisher's bedroom which opened onto it. I tried to ignore the voices but I could not because there was something familiar about their rhythm and pace which tortured me. It was like hearing a tune that for the life of you you can't quite place. I crept to the door of my bedroom and opened it a crack.

The sitting room was empty, but Fisher's bedroom door was open and it was from there that the voices emanated. The clearer of the two voices was Fisher's. What he was saying was still indistinct, but I could recognise it because I knew it so well. It was Roger Tremaine's great speech from the last act of *The Honour of the Tremaines*:

"I say to you, Hubert, that a man's honour is like a precious jewel: once shattered it is never repaired. If a man has honour he will hold it dearer than life itself: for he gives it away at the cost of his immortal soul. Be he the poorest of the poor, the humblest of the humble, if a man has honour, he is a prince among men. But if he has lost it, then, be he as rich as Croesus, as mighty as a king, I declare him to be the vilest dog on earth."

Quite why Fisher should be rehearsing a speech he both knew and performed to perfection was a mystery. But the second voice was an even greater mystery. It seemed to be repeating the speech, though at times it anticipated Fisher. The sound of it was like a muffled groan, only the cadences of the speech being identifiable. It was as if someone or something was struggling to speak with a gag in its mouth.

"I hay to you, Huher, that a han's honour is like a hrehious hewel..."

Who was it? What was happening? I put on my dressing gown and entered the sitting room. As soon as I did so the voices stopped and the door of Fisher's bedroom was slammed shut.

I heard those voices more than once during our week at Castleford, always at our digs, sometimes late at night, sometimes very early in the morning... I wondered at times whether I was dreaming them. Certainly they wove their way into my dreams which were of nameless things, things that were trying to struggle out of miserable dark holes into our world, things which even now I would give all my worldly goods to forget.

As for Fisher, I frankly avoided him. We had

no quarrel; I took my meals with him at the digs, but even then I contrived to be reading a book or otherwise occupied, so that I would not be obliged to exchange too many words with him. I cannot altogether explain my feelings: it was nothing so simple as an aura of wickedness which repelled me. I can best express it by saying that Fisher seemed to me to be living in a different world to ours while still existing in this one. His eyes seemed to focus on points in empty space. He would suddenly address words to no-one in particular. They were often strange words belonging to a language of his own, ugly words of loathing and despair.

"Haaa Gaaa Haaa... No more!"

Of course, it would be easy simply to say that Fisher had gone mad, whatever that may mean, but this would not cover all the facts. In the first place he gave an impeccable performance every night, and if one did speak to him on any subject he would answer as soberly and rationally as ever he did. Only his air of abstraction gave away the fact that a part of him was not attending to you at all.

And so we come to the last fateful night in Castleford. It began for me on a hopeful note.

The matinee had been well received by a capacity house and I was beginning to look forward to the last week of our tour at Darlington where I was determined at all costs not to share digs with Fisher.

After the matinee and before the evening performance I walked out of the theatre to get some fresh air. Fisher had gone out just ahead of me and I saw him walking along the narrow alleyway which led from the stage door to the street, head bowed, muttering something to an invisible presence below him and to his right. He might have been talking to an imaginary dog that trotted by his side. If it was so, the dog was clearly not behaving itself at all well. I waited to see which way he turned into the street, then I took the opposite route.

I returned to the theatre perhaps a little later than I intended, but refreshed, mainly, I think, because I had not seen Fisher. For the first time that week, I felt positively light-hearted. Then, as I walked down the dressing room corridor I became aware of that noise coming from Fisher's dressing room. It was that mumbling gagged voice again which had accompanied Fisher's recitation at the digs...

"I hay to you, Huher, that a han's honour is like a hrehious hewel...

I stopped in my tracks, and all the unspoken horrors of that week threatened to return. I was determined not to let it. I would go and see Fisher and confront him. But with what? I had no idea.

The dressing room door was ajar, I knocked and, receiving no response, I entered. All was silent and the room was empty, but on the table beside the mirror, its back towards me, was the copper wig on the wig block. I looked around more thoroughly and called Fisher's name, but there was no one there. A sensation of moist coldness crept over my skin. My eyes were drawn again to the wig. There were tiny beads of water on it that glistened like diamonds in the gaslight and it seemed almost imperceptibly to be trembling, as if shivering like me from the cold. Yet I could detect no other vibration to account for the movement. I watched transfixed as the wig shuddered almost like a living thing. Then it began to turn around towards me, as an object on a vibrating surface will turn, slowly, hesitantly at first, then with increasing deliberation. Suddenly I felt that of all the things in the world I did not want to see, I did not want to see the blank "face" side of the wig block. I turned and ran from the room.

That was only the first of many strange happenings that night. Before curtain up Miss Manville had hysterics in her dressing room, claiming that she had seen Marden's disembodied head smiling at her in her dressing room mirror. During the performance Fisher seemed distracted. He was constantly adjusting his wig as if it gave him discomfort, and between the second and third acts I saw him drain a large glass of brandy and water in the wings. Not unusual for an actor, you may say, but Fisher was the most abstemious of men and never drank during a show. Neither do I. (*Drinks*)

We reach the last scene of the third act. There are moments on stage when one feels that a scene is not simply being played, but somehow lived by both actors and audience. This was such a moment. I felt as if I were actually in the officer's mess of the Loamshires at Bangrapore. I must have risen to the occasion because when I said: "To any man who says that Roger Tremaine is a blackguard I give the lie!" it was more than usually well received. Normally

Fisher made his entrance as Tremaine with immaculate timing, just as the applause for my line was fading away, but on this night there was a hiatus before he staggered on in his tattered uniform. The pause before Fisher entered seemed horribly long to us on stage, but was probably barely noticed by the audience. "I give the lie myself!" he cried, receiving the usual ovation. Then, instead of crashing dramatically onto the table, Fisher began to reel about clutching at his head. Something had gone hideously amiss. He seemed in agony and his eyes were starting from their sockets. I realised that he was desperately trying to tear his wig off, but to no avail. Little streams of blood began to pour from his temples just where the wig joined Fisher's head. He screamed in agony and, as he did so, a great torrent of blood gushed from under the wig join covering his face, hands and several nearby supers – amateurs – in gore. As he finally crashed onto the table and the curtain fell a great roar of applause burst from the audience. It was Fisher's last and greatest ovation. He never heard it, because, I am convinced, he was dead before he had hit the table.

The last act of the play was cancelled that

night and the Guv'nor went before the curtain to announce that "Upon application at the box office customers' money will be returned." Surprisingly few theatregoers took up this offer, however. I met one in the street the following morning. He told me in his blunt Northern way,

"I've 'ad me shilling's worth!"

No explanation could be discovered for the extraordinary and horrific death of Mr Fisher by either the men of science or of the law. The top of his skull had simply been crushed to a pulp as if it had been a rotten apple. At the inquest a verdict of Death by Misadventure was brought in.

What was the explanation? Officially it remained a mystery. But there was a clue you know to the tragedy. I found it myself. Back at our lodgings on the morning after poor Fisher's death, I just happened to be looking through Fisher's effects. Pure curiosity, you understand. But I came across – now where is it? Ah! – a crumpled piece of paper. (*He takes a piece of paper from his pocket.*) Here. I found it in the grate of his bedroom fireplace. A little burnt at the edges, as you can see. But readable. Still readable.

As you can see, it is a bill, the tradesman in

question being one, "Jabez Wheeler, Superior Wig Maker of 12 Dock Street, Bermondsea." No figures have been written on the bill side of the document, but on the reverse, the following has been scrawled in pencil: "I find there are some additional costs still outstanding. Yours was an unusual request and mine an unusual talent to execute it. I also have a talent for silence, but silence comes at a price. J.W."

Did I inform the authorities? I'm afraid not. I suppose I should have. Dear me. Instead I paid a call upon Mr Jabez Wheeler, Superior Wig Maker of 12 Dock Street, Bermondsea. A most interesting man. Oh, yes. Now you won't believe this but as it happens, I myself was beginning to suffer from – how shall I put it? – a slight thinning at the temples. And Mr Jabez Wheeler was able to accommodate me. Yes, indeed. You see this? (*showing his own hair*) Incredible, isn't it? You wouldn't believe it was a wig. But it is. Oh, yes! Lifelike, isn't it? So lifelike!

Ladies and gentlemen thank you so much for your kind attention. The warder will see you out. And as you exit our little asylum, on the table by the entrance you will find a collecting box in aid of distressed theatrical folk. Please, spare a thought for us, and give generously.

Goodnight, ladies! Goodnight, sweet ladies! Good night! Good night!

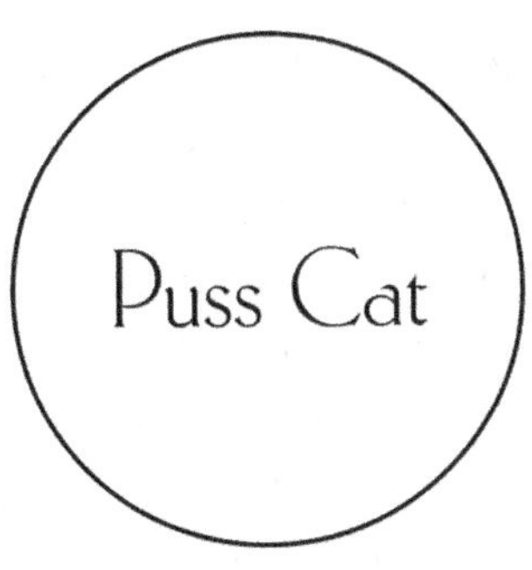

A monologue for an actor

The year is 1980 and Godfrey Jesson, an actor in his sixties, is talking in a quiet bar or hotel lounge, to a younger man, a biographer.

So, you want to know about Sir Roderick Bentley, do you? Well, you've come to the right department, as they say. Thank you, I'll have a large Bell's Whisky, if I may. Plenty of soda. Ice? Good God, no! Yes, Roddy and I went back a long way, to the Old Vic days just after the war. No. No resentment. Roddy was always destined for great things, me for the supporting roles.

"Godders," Roddy said to me once. He always called me "Godders" for some reason, but I prefer to be called Godfrey, if you don't mind.

That's my name. "Godders, you're a good actor. Devilish good, and you'll always be in work. I'll tell you why. You're good but you haven't enough personality to worry a leading man." I'll never forget that. Of course, I suppose I knew he was right, but that doesn't mean to say it wasn't an almighty sock in the jaw.

Well, when Roddy formed his own company, Navigator Productions, he asked me to be in it. Played some good parts – not leads or anything, of course – but I did understudy him quite a bit. In fact I understudied him in his last two productions, and thereby hangs a tale, as they say.

Want to know a funny thing about Roddy? He couldn't stand cats. No, I know on its own that's not particularly strange, but it is odd when you consider that in spite of that he always used to call his girlfriends "puss-cat."

You don't know about the girlfriends? Oh, perhaps I shouldn't have said, but you were bound to find out in the end, weren't you? But you won't mention, will you, in this biography of yours that it was I who told you? I'd hate it to get back to Lady Margery that I said such a thing. I rather doubt that she knows, you see. Or perhaps she does and won't admit it. Women are queer cattle. Ah, the drinks! Well, here's to your book, eh?

Let me make it quite clear: Roddy was devoted to Lady Margery. Devoted. But, you know, when Margery started to have the kids she gave up the theatre. They had this lovely home down in Kent and she didn't like to leave it just to go on tour with him or off to some godforsaken film location in Spain or California. So Roddy had his little adventures, but he always came home.

Now, I know what's going through your mind. I'm not quite the drink-sodden old idiot you think I am, you see. You've got the neat psychological explanation all lined up, haven't you? You think he despised these girlfriends of his, and as he hated cats he called them "puss-cat" out of some subconscious urge to put them down. But it's rather more complicated than that. You see Roddy had three passions in life: the theatre, women and sailing. He had an absolute mania for messing about in boats and, when he became rich and famous, he bought this yacht which was his pride and joy. It was a catamaran, and do you know what he called it?

Yes. "Puss-Cat." So you see it wasn't that simple. Roddy did a lot for his girls one way and another: he brought them on professionally; encouraged them. Some of them have had very good careers thanks to him. No, I'm not going to tell you all their names – you'll have to find that out for yourself – but I'll mention a couple of them perhaps, because they're relevant to what you came to me for. I assume it was the last months of Roddy's life that you wanted me to tell you about?

Thank you. Just another double Bell's with soda and that's my lot. I've always known my limit: key to success, knowing your limits, believe me. By the way, I'll say it just once: this is my version of what happened. Others will tell you different, and it's up to you to decide what the truth of the matter is, because at the end of the day your guess is as good as mine. Probably better actually. After all, you're the writer, aren't you?

Well, the year after Roddy got his "K" and became Sir Roderick, he took out a tour of Pinero's *The Magistrate* and, of course, I was in it. I understudied him and played the nice little role of Wormington. Gets some good laughs in the third act, but you don't want to hear about that, do you? Well naturally Roddy plays the title role of the Magistrate, Posket, and he was superb, believe me.

Do you know *The Magistrate*? It's a good old-fashioned farce. No smut. Never fails: except with the critics, who think it's a bit dusty and dated. That's why we didn't come into the West-End with it, I'm convinced. Well, anyway, in this play there's a rather nice part for a young music teacher called Beatie, and for it, Roddy hires a young unknown actress, name of Yolande Carey. You've heard about her? Well, hold your horses, because believe me, you don't know the half.

Yolande was a sweet little thing, just Roddy's type as it happens. His type? Well, she was slender – "petite", I suppose is the word – blonde with delicate features and a little turned up nose. Looked as if she'd blow away in a light gale. That was Roddy's type. Attraction of opposites, I suppose, because Roddy, as you know, was a big man with one hell of a physique. He was sixty-three at the time I'm talking about but if it wasn't for the grey hair he could have passed for forty five. Don't get the idea though that Roddy picked Yolande just because he fancied her. He wasn't like that. Yolande had talent, believe me – a bit raw, perhaps, and underpowered in the vocal department, but definitely there, and Roddy had spotted it at the audition.

I knew Roddy and I could tell from the start of rehearsals that he fancied her because he gave her such a hard time. Incidentally, Roddy was directing as well as playing the lead. That was not the usual practice, rather archaic, but still done, like the soloist conducting a piano concerto from the keyboard. But, dammit, Gielgud did it, Olivier did it, why not Roddy? He could be a bit of a bully, but on the other hand, he always bullied the ones he cared about most, because he knew they had it in them to give more. Sometimes younger actors found that hard to understand; just as *he* failed to understand that some people just don't respond well to bullying, Yolande being one of them. He kept on at her to project more, throw herself more into the role, until once or twice I could see she was close to tears.

I did my best to reassure Yolande but she thought I was just taking pity on her. When I tried a quiet word with Roddy about it he was very sharp with me, told me to mind my own something something business. I got the impression that he suspected me of being sweet on Yolande, but this wasn't the case. Just to make things clear at the start, I'm gay: not a word I like terribly but the only one available these days. It was a fact about my life that Roddy always chose to ignore. You see, though I don't deny it, I'm not open or obvious about it, and I was actually once married. She left me for a dentist: I won't bore you with the details. Cheers!

Where was I? Yes, well, the Yolande-Roddy situation was resolved in a rather odd way. We were rehearsing for the tour in a run-down old Church Hall in Lambeth. It was a gruesome place, but it was cheap to hire. Roddy, like nearly all theatrical managements I've worked with, could be both very mean and very extravagant in the most unexpected directions, and the Church Hall was one of his false economies. It had Biblical texts on the walls; its windows were dirty; it got us down. It also had a resident cat, an ancient ginger Tom, called Charlie – God knows why I remember that, but I do! – the mangiest old bruiser you ever saw. Charlie had a habit of trotting into rehearsals at odd moments, and standing or sitting very still while he stared at proceedings; then he would start to howl. I think Charlie just wanted to be fed, but we all called him "The Critic", because he did sometimes seem to be commenting on our attempts at comedy.

Needless to say, Roddy loathed Charlie, and one afternoon the animal started howling at a particularly tense moment in rehearsals. Roddy, who was trying to remember lines, lost his temper completely, rushed at Charlie and gave him the most almighty kick. Charlie let out an awful screech and Yolande, who was standing nearby, ran to pick him up. She was the only one of us who had shown any sort of soft spot for Charlie, the Critic. She cuddled the wretched old beast in her arms and absolutely tore a strip off Roddy for what he had done. Roddy stared at her in amazement. He said nothing, and I could see his mind working. Once I saw his mouth twitch into a smile, but he controlled himself. Having heard her out in silence he simply and graciously apologised to her. He said that what he had done was "unpardonable." Yolande released Charlie, who had been clawing and struggling in her arms in the most ungrateful way. He dashed off and was never seen again.

That incident marked a turning point in relations between Roddy and Yolande. Her acting became bolder and more confident; Roddy's criticisms became more muted. They ceased to be boss and junior employee and became colleagues. It was a great relief all round.

I don't exactly know when their affair started, but I think it was fairly early on in the tour, and I suspect it was our second week, which was the Theatre Royal, Newcastle. Do you know it? Lovely old theatre.

On the Tuesday morning Yolande and I happened to meet Roddy at the stage door. We had just been in to see if there was any mail for us and, as it was a fine April day, we were standing outside talking about nothing in particular when Roddy appeared. I could see he was in one of his restless moods, and on the spur of the moment he proposed to take us out on a jaunt. He was going to show us Hadrian's Wall, an idea which seemed to thrill Yolande, but me less so – I'd been. However I went because it was clear from Roddy's look that he wanted me there. I wasn't quite sure why, but, you know, Roddy was a compulsive performer and liked an audience for practically everything he did, even seduction.

We drove out of Newcastle and followed the wall. It was one of those soft, mild days of spring, full of haze and new bird song when the pale green of the hills blended with the grey ribs and ridges of Roman wall and fortress. Yolande listened to Roddy with the rapt wonder of a schoolgirl as he explained the wall to her. We got out at Housesteads, the best preserved fort on the wall, and wandered about, almost the only people there. At one point Yolande asked about Hadrian himself, what sort of man was he? Roddy who, outside military history and dates, was less well informed, hesitated. So I gave them an account of the only thing I knew about Hadrian, his passion for the glamorous youth Antinous whose mysterious death blighted the Emperor's later years. Yolande was puzzled.

"I didn't know they had gays in those days," she said. Roddy, who was standing behind her, looked at me and winked. I ignored him and went into some rubbish about the Greeks and Plato and Socrates. For the rest of the time we were out I felt very uneasy. Roddy was flirting with Yolande and completely ignoring me, while she was laughing at everything he said in that way people do when they meet Royalty or fall in love.

He drove us back to the theatre. At the stage door I noticed that the theatre cat, a black, green-eyed streak of feline cunning, had stretched out its lean body on the door step to catch the weak Newcastle sun. When he saw it, Roddy did a thing I'd never seen him do before. He crouched down and tentatively tickled the animal's stomach.

"Hello, puss-cat," he said with a rather unconvincing show of bonhomie. The cat ignored him, and Roddy looked up at Yolande.

He said: "I wonder, old thing. I'm going back to my hotel. I've got to look over that bit in the third act where I got in such a tangle last night. Remember? You wouldn't be an absolute brick and come back with me for a cuppa and test me on my lines, would you?"

There was a little pause, just long enough for it to be made obvious that she knew what he meant and he knew that she knew, and, well, you know the rest. I thought for a moment she was going to turn him down rather huffily, but she didn't; she simply said: "Okay," and off they went.

I'm pretty sure that was the beginning of things, because after that one would often see them together in the wings or in the dressing room corridors, just talking. They weren't touching or anything obvious like that and I'm sure they thought they were being incredibly discreet, but very soon the rumours were flying around. You know how these things are picked up amazingly quickly by a company on tour with nothing much to do except gossip about each other.

One thing that one of the other actresses in the company said stuck in my mind. She said: "I wonder what would happen if Bel knew." Bel of course was Belinda Courteney. Yes, *the* Belinda Courteney. Yes, she was one of Roddy's girls at one time, but don't tell her I told you. I'm up for an interview for the National next week and you know how her writ runs there. As a matter of fact, I thought the Bel Courteney affair was over, but apparently some thought otherwise.

Yolande occasionally confided in me. I suppose I was a safe pair of hands, and she knew I knew, so to speak. I tried to sound kindly and wise: you know how one slips into these roles, especially if one is an actor. I was dear old Uncle

Godfrey to her, and, I'm afraid, to me too in those moments. Yolande was a sweet thing, but such a child. She had become obsessed by Roddy and used to ask me about every detail of his career, the books he liked, the food he preferred, everything. I honestly think she thought he was going to leave Lady Margery for her. She said: "You know he hasn't slept with her for eight years." I refrained from saying that that was what he told all the girls, because it was only a guess, but perhaps I should have done.

Well, the tour wound up fairly successfully in October at the Theatre Royal Richmond, traditionally one of those "last date before the West End" venues, but it was not to be. There had been talk of a West End Theatre several times in the tour, but it came to nothing. With such a huge cast we needed a thousand seater plus just to break even and all the big houses were stubbornly full of American musicals that year.

So the company disbanded, but Yolande and I kept in touch, partly because I sensed she needed someone to talk to about Roddy. Most of her other friends wouldn't have understood. They were non-theatrical and, frankly, just a bit odd. They tended to call themselves "aromatherapists", "Feng Shui consultants", "musicians", "spiritual healers": all those euphemisms by which the barely employable salve the wound of their uselessness. Forgive me, my prejudice is showing; it must be the Bell's.

She had a little flat above a patisserie in the St John's Wood High Street. She'd ask me round at odd times of the day for a cup of herb tea and, if I was lucky, a slice of carrot cake, but the subject of conversation was always the same: Roddy. They were still seeing each other, and he used occasionally to take her away for weekends in Paris or Torquay – his boat was down at Torquay, you see – but after one or two visits he wouldn't come to her flat any more. The excuse he gave was that he was allergic to her cat, and one can't altogether blame him. I'm not myself averse to cats, but this one of Yolande's, a rescued stray, was not a notably attractive specimen. It was an elderly neutered Tom, brindled, with a sagging belly and a passion for tinned sardines. Yolande, you see, was one of those people who is instantly drawn to anything even more defenceless than herself.

Rather unwisely I think, Yolande called the cat Roddy. I don't know whether she actually addressed the cat as such in the other Roddy's presence, but it would explain his allergy if she did.

I was managing to keep myself alive by the odd voice over, and a beer commercial, but by the end of November Yolande was beginning to be rather uncomfortably out of work. She had some sort of part time employment at a nearby book shop which didn't bring in much, but it wasn't just the money. Acting is a drug: once you become addicted, you need a regular fix. Yolande told me that Roddy had offered to "lend" her some money which she had indignantly refused, and he was beginning to see less of her. In December he went away for some filming in Spain; then just before Christmas something happened which lifted her out of the gloom she was falling into. She had a Christmas Card from Roddy, and there was a message in it.

Excitedly she asked me round for herb tea to see the card. She wouldn't say anything more on the phone, so I came. I had barely taken a sip of Dandelion and Camomile – a filthy concoction, take my word, don't go near the stuff – before she had thrust the Actor's Benevolent Fund card into my hand. Inside it read as follows:

"Darling Puss-Cat,

"Filming here nearly over. Shan't be sorry. Ghastly Spanish food swimming in oil. Fell off a horse yesterday in full armour. No joke. Puss-Cat, I'm taking out a Spring Tour of King Lear next year and I've done a deal which guarantees us a West End Theatre. The long and the short of it is I want you to be my Cordelia. What say you?

"Your ever loving,

"Roddy"

I have to confess that my first reaction was a typical actor's one: jealousy. He was taking out a tour of King Lear and there were plenty of parts for me – Kent, perhaps even Gloucester – why hadn't Roddy been in touch about it? But this was no time to feel hurt; Yolande was asking me what she should do. I said it was obvious. She should get her agent to contact the Navigator Productions office and accept the offer. Yolande said she had already done that.

Then there was a long laborious discussion in which she went on about her utter inadequacy for the role – she had never done Shakespeare professionally – and I, as I was expected to do, reassured her that she would make a splendid Cordelia. I thought it might be tactless to remark that one of her main qualifications for the part was the fact that she was a light girl, only just over seven stone. The elderly actor playing Lear, you see, must carry Cordelia on stage at the end of the play, so weight is a consideration, especially in a long run, and it was one of which I am sure Roddy had been mindful.

Well, that seemed to be that. I didn't hear much from Yolande till after Christmas. Then she began to be a bit worried because Roddy had not been in touch with her. This was the arrangement, you see. She was not allowed to ring him in case Lady Margery answered the phone: he would always call her. More worrying perhaps than that, there had been no response from the Navigator Productions office about her acceptance of Cordelia. This puzzled me because by this time my agent had been notified that Roddy was "interested" in me for the part of Kent.

Early in January Roddy asked me over to the Navigator Offices just off the Charing Cross Road to "talk about Kent." I knew this amounted to a firm offer, so I went eagerly and found him welcoming and friendly as always, but, I thought, a little distracted. We discussed the production and my part which he described as "hell's important" and "absolutely key." We also discussed the salary he was offering. He apologised profusely that it couldn't be higher; in fact he seemed so distressed about it that in the end *I* began to feel guilty, as if I had gone in asking for more money than he could afford which, of course, I hadn't. In the end, to relieve the tension, I said:

"I gather Yolande is going to be your Cordelia."

Roddy's reaction was most unexpected. He looked at me with a shocked, almost fearful expression, as if something poisonous had just bitten him.

"What the hell are you on about, Godders?" he said.

Now, I didn't want to admit that I'd read a private Christmas card so I was a bit vague at first, but Roddy simply didn't understand. In the end I had to tell him explicitly that she had shown me the message from him. Even then, it was quite some time before he reacted. Then it was as if a flash from a bolt of lightning had suddenly bleached his face.

Roddy said: "Oh, my God! Oh, my Christ! Oh, my golly gosh!" Then, after a long pause, he said in a quiet, thoughtful sort of a way: "Oh, fuck!"

I waited patiently for the explanation. At last he sighed, as if these things had been sent to try him and he told me:

"I wrote all my bloody Christmas cards in Spain. I thought it would be something to do. You know the waiting around that goes on, especially when you're filming one of these ghastly Hollywood Epics. I can remember writing all the cards, then I got a tummy bug from some fearful Spanish muck they served us. Well, the doc, under instructions from the director of course, just drugged me up to the eyeballs so I could get onto that bloody horse again. It was while I was under the influence that I did the envelopes for the cards. I do vaguely remember doing Bel Courteney's at the same time as Yolande's..."

I got his drift. "You mean the offer of Cordelia was meant for Belinda Courteney? You put the card in the wrong envelope?"

"Yes. Dammit! Yes! I've been wondering why

Bel hadn't responded. In fact... Oh, buggeration and hell!"

He seemed even more upset than before and I asked him what was the matter. At last I got it out of him that the card he had intended for Yolande contained a suggestion, couched in the gentlest possible terms, that perhaps in future they might be seeing rather less of each other than before.

I said: "You mean, you might have sent the brush off for Yolande to Belinda by mistake as well?" Roddy started rubbing his face with his hands so he wouldn't have to look at me. By this time, I was almost as upset as he was. I said: "But you called her puss-cat."

"Who?"

"Yolande – I mean Belinda."

"Yes. Yes! They're all called puss-cat." He seemed very irritated that I had brought the matter up. Then he became all abject and apologetic which was almost worse. He said: "Look, Godfrey, dear old thing, would you do me the most enormous favour? Would you try to break all this to Yolande? And do it gently, won't you, dear old boy. I know you will. You're such a brick. The fact is I just can't face it at the moment. I'm up to here with Lear, as you can imagine, and I've got to try and sort things out with Belinda."

I said: "Are you sure you wouldn't like me to tackle *her* as well?"

Roddy didn't react; he just shook his head solemnly. "No thanks. That's awfully decent, but I have to do that myself." My attempts at irony have always fallen on deaf ears. Not so much *esprit de l'escalier* as *esprit de corpse,* eh? Oh, never mind. So I agreed to see Yolande for him. Of course I agreed. You can't just fall out of love with someone after forty years. At least, I can't.

I thought of telling Yolande by phone or even a letter, but in the end I decided to go to see her: it seemed the only decent thing to do. Well, we got sat down with the herb tea and everything and the cat Roddy purring on her lap and I began to explain. It was horrible because she found it so hard to take it in. I had to say everything twice. She didn't rage, or throw things, or spit with hatred or anything – I would have preferred that – she just listened with a baffled expression on her face. There were no sobs, but her eyes were wet with tears. She kept saying: "But why? Does he hate me or something?" And I said "No," very loudly and firmly, because I was sure he didn't. Then she asked me to explain about the card yet again, so I did.

She nodded a few times before she said: "So he doesn't want me to be his Cordelia?"

I shook my head. There was a bit of a pause, then she came out with something which jolly nearly broke me up. She said: "I'd started learning the lines."

Oh, God! You wouldn't understand, would you? You're not an actor.

Well, we began work on Lear and I rather lost touch with Yolande. Rehearsals were engrossing and I had the feeling she would not want to hear about them. Incidentally, Belinda Courteney did not play Cordelia – it was the year of her groundbreaking Hedda Gabler at the National – and the girl who did was no better and no worse than Yolande might have been. Roddy was on top form as Lear and I think everyone who saw him agrees that he gave the performance of his life. The rest of the cast was good, the set was functional and, though the costumes belonged to the then fashionable "Ruritanian Stalinist" school, they did at least fit. We opened fairly triumphantly in, of all places, Blackpool.

There was a six week pre-West End tour and I must admit that I completely forgot about Yolande until the last week at Cardiff when, half an hour before curtain up on the Thursday, I was summoned through the loudspeaker in my dressing room to the phone at the stage door. There was a call for me.

It was one of Yolande's odd friends – the aromatherapist, I think – and how she had managed to track me down to the Theatre Royal Cardiff, I do not know. She told me that the previous day the couple in the flat above Yolande's had heard this howling and scratching on the door of Yolande's flat, obviously the wretched cat Roddy in some distress. They tried calling Yolande but got no reply. To cut a long story short, the police were summoned and when they broke down the door, they found Yolande lying on the bed, dead. She'd taken enough barbiturates to kill a horse. Roddy the cat had gone frantic with hunger and everything and the place stank of his poo, but he hadn't touched Yolande's body.

I went through the performance that night in a daze, wondering when and how I should tell Roddy. In the end I funked it altogether.

The following evening, I was standing in the wings waiting to go on and begin the play when I became aware of Roddy lurking behind me.

He said: "You've heard about Yolande?" I nodded. He said: "I've been rather knocked endways by it all. The Company Office rang and told me this afternoon. Someone there had seen a paragraph in the Evening Standard. I can't understand it, can you?"

I shook my head.

"I mean, I know she was out of work and all that, but... She must have had some sort of mental trouble. A breakdown. Terrible. She was a dear, sweet thing. Not without talent." There was a pause, then he said: "You know, Godders, I hate to say it, but young people today, they don't seem to have the backbone. They give up too easily. I mean, we've all had our bad patches in this profession, God knows, but you need a bit of grit and spunk to stick to it. Don't you agree?" To my shame I nodded and Roddy gave me a great bear hug.

The next minute the lights had gone up on stage and I was striding into another world as Kent and uttering the first words of the play: "I thought the King had more affected the Duke of Albany than Cornwall."

Roddy never mentioned Yolande again in my presence, but I believe there was a moment that night at the end of the play when perhaps he remembered her. It came in the final scene when he is on the ground, lamenting over the dead body of Cordelia and I am in attendance, and he says the words:

"A plague upon you, murderers, traitors all!

I might have saved her; now she's gone for ever."

At that moment he did something he'd never done before, he looked up at me. There were tears in his eyes, and they were not stage tears. I like to think they weren't.

So we moved to our London venue, the Irving Theatre in The Strand, for a limited run of three months, and the critics fortunately decided that Roddy was a great Lear. All the same, after the exhilaration of the tour when we were all discovering how good the show was, the West End run seemed to be a bit flat, and, of course, because in London most of the cast had their own homes to go to and their own lives to lead, some of the camaraderie in the company went too.

I didn't particularly like the Irving. It's big, draughty old Victorian building, perhaps even a little sinister, and it had, of course, a theatre cat. They're vital things you know, because theatres get rats, and rats gnaw cables, and gnawed electric cables start fires, especially in theatres. The Irving cat was a black Tom called Nimrod, not a very sociable beast, but, as befitted his name, a "mighty hunter before the Lord" who kept the rats and mice down very effectively. But here's a funny thing: about a week into our run Nimrod disappeared.

The theatre manager was very distressed and offered a reward for his discovery and return. There was even a bit in the papers about it. I wouldn't have mentioned this only it may have a bearing on what happened next.

Fortunately, the disappearance of Nimrod did not result in a rodent invasion. In fact – and this was something that puzzled many of us – the odd half eaten rat or mouse could still be found in odd corners of the theatre, if anything with more frequency than before Nimrod's vanishing act. These grisly remains, which had been left around by Nimrod as tokens of his prowess, were now nearly always to be found either in the wings or in the corridor leading to Dressing Room Number 1, Roddy's of course. In fact Roddy came in one day for a matinee to find a headless rat carefully placed on the very threshold of Number 1. He made a terrific fuss about that, as he had every right to, of course, but I thought there was a touch of hysteria in his manner which was uncharacteristic. He didn't usually play the Prima Donna.

A couple of days later Roddy happened to meet me back stage in the interval and invited me to his dressing room for a whisky. The one he poured himself was unusually large. He'd never been a boozer, and certainly not during a show. He seemed to be under some sort of strain.

Having sat me down, he said: "Now then, Godders, what are we going to do about this cat business?" I looked blank. He said: "Don't tell me you haven't noticed this damned cat which keeps following me around the theatre?"

I said that I hadn't seen any cat and anyway – didn't he know? – Nimrod had disappeared. Roddy banged his glass impatiently down on the dressing table.

"Yes! Yes! I know all about Nimrod. That dam' theatre manager is obsessed with Nimrod. I didn't mind Nimrod. He kept out of your way and did his job. This is a different cat altogether. It won't leave me alone. It keeps coming up to me just as I'm going on stage and purring, and doing that thing that cats do, you know, curling itself round your legs. It nearly tripped me up the other day just as I was going on for 'Blow Winds!' It's a blasted nuisance. And it keeps leaving these offerings for me in my dressing room. You know, bits of disembowelled rat and mouse. I trod on an intestine with my bare foot the other day as I was changing. Ugh! I can't think how the bugger gets in. I always lock my dressing room when I go. I suppose it must be the cleaners. I've spoken to the manager about it but he hasn't a clue. He's so obsessed about Nimrod I don't think he believes in this other cat."

I asked what it looked like.

"Funny sort of colour. I don't know. Greyish, I think, but these sort of yellow eyes which look as if they light up in the dark. You know how some cats seem to have luminous eyes. It's difficult to tell exactly what it looks like because I haven't seen it in full light. It usually turns up in the wings, just outside the glare of the stage lights. I wouldn't mind only – I know this is a funny thing to say – it's so damned fond of me. It's obsessed. It's like, you know, some creepy sort of stalker. Godders, you must have seen it."

There was pleading in his voice, but I had to confess that I hadn't. To reassure him I said I said I would keep "a weather eye" open for it. He liked that: a nautical expression, you see, "weather eye."

In the final scene that night an odd thing happened. Lear has come on with the dead body of Cordelia and we're standing around. Roddy, was doing pretty well, but not on top form, I thought. He kept looking off stage. Then comes his final speech when he is lamenting over the dead Cordelia and he says:

"Why should a dog, a horse, a rat have life,
And thou no breath at all?"

Except that this night he doesn't quite say that, he says:

"Why should a dog, a horse, a *cat* have life,
And thou no breath at all?"

And his eyes are fixed on something off stage right in the wings. Well, I couldn't resist looking there myself. I was half dazzled by the stage lights so I can't be sure, but do you know for a second or two somewhere in the gloom I thought I did catch sight of two yellow cat's eyes staring at the action on stage. Well, I can't be sure because I had to get back to my job. I still had lines to say, but when I'd said my last ones – you remember—

"I have a journey, sir, shortly to go;
My master calls me, I must not say no."

—I look back into the wings, and there's nothing there. The eyes had gone.

Next day was a matinee day and before the first house Roddy summoned me to his dressing room. He seemed very excited.

He said: "I think I've got the answer to our little problem. You see this?" He held up a transparent plastic phial, the kind you pee into for doctors. It had about a centimetre of white powder in it. "Know what that is?" He didn't wait for my answer. "Strychnine. Don't ask me how I got it. Had to pull a few strings. One of the few advantages of being "Sir Roderick" is that you can occasionally pull a string or two. I'm going to put it in some milk and put the milk in a saucer in my dressing room and when that dam' cat comes, it is going to drink that milk. All cats like milk, don't they?"

I said I was no expert, but I understood that cats liked milk.

He said: "Right! That dam' cat's going to die and all our troubles are over!"

I couldn't help feeling that Roddy had got things rather out of proportion, but he seemed exhilarated and that afternoon a slightly sparse audience got the performance of a lifetime. By the end of it Roddy was clearly exhausted, which worried me, but something was keeping him alight. He seemed – what's the word I'm looking for? – febrile, that's it, and it worried me.

That was why I decided to look in on him in his dressing room just before the half hour call for the evening show. I knocked on the door which was slightly ajar but got no reply, so I looked in.

Roddy had not got out of his last act costume or his make-up. He was lying on the floor of his dressing room, arms outstretched. He didn't look to me as if he was breathing. Beside him on the floor was an empty bowl. At the corners of his half open mouth were little droplets of liquid which looked to me like milk.

But that was not the worst of it. Crouched on his chest was the biggest damned cat I've ever seen in my life. Its fur was shaggy and grey – it looked like a great ball of dirty smoke – and its angry eyes were a bright sulphur yellow. Slowly it arched its back and gave me a low, sterterous hiss like the sudden escape of steam from an engine under pressure.

You don't believe me? Well, that's my story and I'm sticking to it.

I ran to get the Company Stage Manager and when we got back to Number One dressing room, Roddy was still there on the floor, but the cat had gone. We phoned an ambulance and they carted him off to hospital but it wasn't any good. He was dead as mutton: heart failure apparently. I said nothing about the strychnine business because I thought it would only muddy the waters, and it probably wasn't relevant.

That night, for the first and last time in my life, I went on for Roddy as King Lear. Did I tell you I was his understudy? Made a pretty good fist of it too, though I says it as shouldn't. Standing ovation and all that.

"Godders," Roddy used to say to me, "you're a good actor. Devilish good, but you haven't enough personality to worry a leading man." I wonder if he'd think that now, eh? What? Another Bell's? Oh, all right, just this once, since you're twisting my arm. Cheers!

The Skins

I first met Syd and Peggy Brinton in August 1977 on the Sunday after Elvis Presley died.

It was a sultry evening at the Pier Pavilion Theatre, Scarmouth and an argument was simmering before the show in No 5. dressing room which Victor Bright and I occupied. We had come in early that day to gorge ourselves on images of the doomed star in our shared Sunday papers. Details about hamburgers and drugs, the distended, tawdry glamour of Graceland, were pored over with sickened fascination. Thinking of that mountain of flesh, now cold and corrupting, I felt a strange, guilty satisfaction: I would never know such stardom; but I would equally never know the futility of success, or its ignominious end.

To purge myself of these unworthy thoughts,

I gave way to pious platitudes. "What a waste!" I said. "That fantastic talent. It's just such a waste…"

Victor, who loved to pick a fight, took the opposite view. Of course it wasn't a waste; it was the inevitable end. Elvis was finished, had been finished for years. He had done what he was meant to do: changed the face of modern music. He had nowhere else to go, nothing to do except give increasingly pathetic displays of his spent talent. Dying was the best thing he could have done. He ought to have died sooner.

I rose to the bait and was beginning to challenge Victor when there was a knock at the door. It opened a fraction and two smiling heads popped round it simultaneously, a male and a female.

"Hello," they said, almost in unison. "We're Syd and Peggy. We're the new Spesh!" The next instant they were gone.

It had all been done with such precision, such show business flair, it had come as if on cue at such a critical moment, that the tension was immediately relieved and both of us burst out laughing. So they were Syd and Peggy Brinton, the new Spesh.

The "Spesh", or Speciality Act, was a feature of our Sunday nights at the Pier Pavilion, Scarmouth. During the week we performed in a couple of plays, a comedy and a thriller, changing midweek, but on Sunday, the night when we regularly filled the theatre, there was "Old Tyme Music Hall with Special Guest Stars", two of whom were Syd and Peggy.

They came to us nearly at the end of the season because the management, "Bunny G. Enterprises", had a violent disagreement with the previous "Spesh", an Ultra Violet Puppet act called "Fantastique!" We were not sorry to see it go because the two men who were "Fantastique!" gave themselves airs. They thought they were better than us lowly actors; they called themselves artists rather than "artistes". Entertainment, not art, was what Bunny G. Enterprises was about and Syd and Peggy Brinton had similar priorities.

Their bill material was "Syd and Peggy Brinton, Comedy Tap Sensation." Their act, always a precise and theatrically correct twenty minutes, began with "Happy Feet" and ended with "Me and My Shadow". Between these two numbers, the tap-dancing elements of their performance, they executed a harmless and fairly ordinary magic act involving balloons and mild comic banter. Their routine never varied and was always well if not enthusiastically received.

I had watched them from the side that night and enjoyed their performance. Syd had winked at me once through his sweat as they clicked and shuffled round the stage to "Happy Feet". Peggy had barmaid blonde looks, a good figure and excellent legs. At five foot five, Syd was no more than an inch taller, lithe and slightly wizened. They seemed to my young eyes pretty ancient but they were only in their mid-forties. He wore a dinner jacket, she a gold lamé leotard and fishnet tights; both carried straw boaters and canes for their numbers.

I saw them in the theatre bar after the performance. Syd stood at the bar with the boss, Mr. Warren "Bunny" Goldman, who had come down specially to see them into the show. Syd was laughing uproariously at Bunny's jokes, as one had to, but I noticed that Peggy was sitting alone at a distant table sipping from a schooner of sweet sherry. The rest of the company were ignoring her for some reason. When our eyes met I felt compelled to go over and keep her company and I saw relief in her smile as I joined her. Close to, her face, still carrying a heavy stage make-up, looked quite deeply lined. She fished in her bag, took out a packet of cigarettes and offered me one. I declined and she lit up with a quick, almost convulsive movement.

"I enjoyed the act," I said.

"Yes. We spotted you in the wings there. Did you really like it?"

"Isn't it terrible about Elvis?" she said after a slight pause. I nodded. She went on: "It's terrible the things they're saying about him in the papers now he's dead. I'm sure none of them are true. He had a lovely act. Syd used to do an Elvis impersonation in the routine. We couldn't do it now of course."

I was intrigued. As a young actor in "legit" theatre I had very little understanding of the variety side of things and was curious to know more about it.

"Mostly we do the clubs and guest appearances like this," she told me. "We have done summer season variety, but we like the clubs. We always go down well in the clubs. It's a clean act: I think they like that for a change.

There's a lot of blue material in the clubs these days. Yes, it's a good act. But there's always room for improvement, isn't there? That's what I say. I keep telling Syd. We ought to change now and then. Put in more gags. We've got to move with the times. But he's happy as it is. He won't budge. Typical man. We could be a topflight supporting act. We've done it before. Once we closed the first half for Frankie Laine at the Empire, Hartlepool, you know. We're very big in Hartlepool."

I looked impressed and asked her if they worked the clubs all the year round.

"Oh, no! We're always in Panto at Christmas. We do the skins, you see."

I must have looked blank, so she explained. "We're in the skins. Like Pantomime Horse. And Daisy the Cow, you know. They call it the skins. People don't understand, but it's a very specialised field. Not just anyone can do it. Our feature is a tap routine in the skins. It's famous. We're one of the top skins double acts in the country. Of course, you know, the great skins role in panto is a single. It's *Mother Goose*. You've got a real character there in Priscilla the Goose. You have to do pathos and everything. She's central to the subject, you see; lays the golden eggs. I could do that. I haven't yet because of Syd. He wouldn't have a role, you see. So it's Daisy and Dobbin for us." She sighed resentfully and pulled hard on her cigarette.

Over the course of the next few Sundays I had several talks with Peggy. She and Syd always seemed on amicable terms but, as if by some unspoken ritual, they never drank together in the bar after the show. Peggy liked to talk but she did not have Syd's natural gregariousness. "Syd's a man's man, you see," she said to me once when we heard his loud laugh above the others at the bar. I gathered that she and Syd had teamed up and married early. They had one son, Mick, who was grown up and in work "Stage Managing at the London Palladium." Peggy was inordinately proud of this. "He's doing really well there," she would say. When I asked what position he occupied in the stage management hierarchy she was vague, but she said that he got on really well with everyone and "they all love Mick."

I found that few people in the company cared to spend time with Peggy. I couldn't quite see why. Victor in particular took against her: he objected to her smoking. "That's bad enough," he said. "One has to look after one's voice. But she will wave the bloody cigarette around in that twitchy way." Admittedly too, her conversational range was limited. She really only had two subjects: their son Mick and their professional status. She would often tell me how they were one of the top skins acts in the country and that her great ambition was to play Priscilla in *Mother Goose*.

On the last Sunday of the season there was a party in the bar afterwards; the drinks were on Bunny Goodman and everyone got a little drunk. I remember once again finding myself with Peggy, who had abandoned her strict rule of one schooner of sherry per night and was on her fourth or fifth. She told me twice about how they had closed the first half for Frankie Laine in Hartlepool, then suddenly and quite unexpectedly she seized my knee under the table in a strong nervous grip.

With little relevance to what had gone before she fixed me with a stare and said: "Don't get me wrong. Syd's all right. I'm not complaining. But he doesn't satisfy me. You know what I mean? I need to be satisfied." I saw her hazel eyes begin to flood with tears. Those eyes were the only real thing about her face: the rest was green eye shadow, false lashes, lip gloss, Max Factor pancake and powder. It was like a mask, or another skin.

Then, just as suddenly, she released my knee and began to apologise abjectly. I found this as embarrassing as what had gone before, so I made excuses and left her as soon as I could.

~

At Christmas a couple of years later, having nothing better to go to, I accepted an offer from Bunny to play Will Scarlett, one of the Merry Men, in *Babes in the Wood* at the Alhambra, Brightsea. Victor Bright was playing the Sheriff of Nottingham and since we had last worked together he had become a "name". He had landed the role of one of those ruthless yet virile businessmen, so beloved of TV Soaps, in a thing called *Seaways*. So he was near the top of the bill as "Victor Bright, TV's Mr Nasty." Also in the cast were Syd and Peggy Brinton who, in addition to being "Merry Men", were in the skins as "Dobbin, the Wonderhorse." At the first rehearsal Peggy greeted me pleasantly but quite distantly. I wondered whether she remembered our intimate conversations at Scarmouth, or whether she had chosen to forget them. Victor Bright was similarly aloof, but for different reasons. Success had clad him in a hard, shiny carapace of invulnerability.

We opened on Boxing Day. It was a good show and there was talk of "breaking all box office records," something which is done more frequently than you might imagine. To me everyone seemed happy, but I was wrong: I do not have the kind of sensitivities which detect what is going on in a company.

About a week into the run I happened to be in the wings watching Syd and Peggy as Dobbin the horse doing their tap dance. I regularly watched it from the side as it was a most expert performance. Peggy took the front half of the horse and Syd the rear. Suddenly I became aware of Freddie Dring, our Dame, gigantic in a white frock covered in huge red polka dots, standing beside me. He was waiting to make his entrance.

"That's a very Biblical Horse you've got there, my friend," he said, nudging me in the groin with a vast purple handbag. On and off stage

Freddie Dring spoke almost entirely in gags, so I knew what was expected of me.

"Oh, and why is that a Biblical Horse?" I said, feeding him the punch line.

"Because the back legs knoweth not what the front legs doeth."

"Oh, I don't know," I said. "I think they're amazingly co-ordinated. And that dance—"

But Freddie cut me off. "Don't be green, son. Don't be green," he said and made his entrance.

It often happens that when you get wind of trouble from one source it is almost immediately confirmed from another. During the interval I happened to overhear a conversation between the two actresses playing Principal Girl and Principal Boy. They had gone for a smoke just outside the stage door.

"Bastard!" said Robin Hood. "He thinks he's God's gift. I told him when he tried to put a hand up my tunic, 'My boyfriend's a Black Belt and he's taught me a move or two.'"

"Is he?" asked Maid Marian. "A Black Belt?"

"No. He's a Chartered Surveyor. But he was in the Territorials. You know who Mr Wonderful's trying it on with now?"

"No! Who?"

"Dobbin."

"No! Front or back?"

Robin Hood let out a snort of laughter. "Oh, Please! One thing he's *not* is a wrong ender."

"Be a lot less trouble if he were if you ask me," said Maid Marian, who was newly married and had a philosophical approach to life. "But that is *so* disgusting! Peggy! I mean she's... Just because he's been in some poxy soap he thinks he's God's Gift. What's Peggy doing about it?"

Robin Hood said: "You won't believe this—" But just then she saw me and drew Maid Marian away to share further secrets, unspied on.

I had heard enough, and next day a fresh piece of news was all over the company. Syd had caught Peggy and Victor "at it" in Peggy and Syd's camper van in the theatre car park. "I tell you, he wouldn't have minded only they were doing terrible things to the suspension," said Freddie Dring.

That evening we saw Peggy and Syd enter the theatre, silent, tight-lipped. An equally taciturn Victor played the Sheriff of Nottingham with such venom that several terrified young members of the audience had to be removed from the auditorium. When it was time for

Dobbin to do its tap dance most of the company was gathered on the side of the stage to watch the spectacle.

It seemed a monstrous thing that clattered and stamped its way about the stage that night. Syd and Peggy, consummate professionals, were giving their usual well-drilled performance, but perhaps their steps were more percussive than usual, their taps more brutally metallic. Every ripple of the shabby cloth skin, every nod of the clumsy beast's head seemed a sign of the terrible, claustrophobic conflict that must be raging within. Freddie, who might have been expected to come up with something humorous, was in a gloomy mood. "I tell you," he said. "There's worse to come. I've never liked *Babes in the Wood* as a subject. It's always been a jinxed panto. It's a well-known fact."

~

The following morning I was summoned to the theatre. Syd had had an accident after the previous night's performance; he had injured his leg badly and was in hospital. The cause of the accident was not vouchsafed to me: I was there because Peggy had selected me to take over the back legs of Dobbin while Syd was out of action. I knew that any protest on my part would not be tolerated because Bunny Goldman had driven down from London and was sitting stony faced in the auditorium.

Peggy seemed unnaturally calm. She said that "everyone" had thought it would be a shame to remove Dobbin altogether from the pantomime, but that I would not be expected to do anything too difficult, like the tap dance. From now until the first show at 2.30 Peggy was to give me a crash course in "working the skins."

It was a strange, uncomfortable time which Peggy handled better than I. Perhaps the concentration required in giving instructions to a novice purged her mind of other, more troublesome thoughts. And I was in the acutely embarrassing position of having to enter Syd's skin.

Nothing quite prepares you for the experience of being "in the skins". You are not entirely in the dark because gauzes set into the cloth give you glimpses of the stage, but the sense of entrapment and enclosure is astonishingly intense. The feeling was enhanced for me because I was acutely conscious of occupying another's space. The smell inside was not particularly offensive but it was somehow personal to the body which had once occupied it, and the body of the former occupant's partner which still did. I felt an acute and irrational terror of touching Peggy in the skins.

Before I made my first entrance in this new role Freddie Dring winked at me and said: "Sooner you than me mate. Talk about dancing cheek to cheek, eh? Eh?"

"We're not doing the dance," I said solemnly.

"Don't be green, son. Don't be green," said Freddie.

I thought that, all things considered, the matinee performance did not go badly. I performed as instructed by Peggy and was hoping for some word of commendation at the end of it. Instead, when we had taken off the skins for the last time I was met with a set face and an angry stare.

"When you're in the skins, you keep your hands to yourself. That's one of the golden rules. I thought every professional knew that. Don't you ever do that again."

I was astonished. I had avoided any physical contact with her whatsoever. The last thing I had wanted to do was touch her. My protests and denials were cut short.

"Don't insult me by lying, young man!" she said as she stalked off to her dressing room carrying the empty horse.

~

Between the matinee and the evening show I visited Syd in hospital. I had learned that the night before, after the show, Syd had wandered off and got drunk. On his way back to the camper van late at night he had lurched out into the road and was run over by a car. His right leg was badly damaged; how badly I did not yet know. There had been conflicting opinions among the company, some saying that he would be out of hospital and dancing in a matter of days, others offering less hopeful prognostics.

Syd occupied a private room in the hospital. I found him sitting up in bed surrounded by flowers, fruit and Get Well cards. His right leg was under a frame which formed a long barrow in the blanketed surface of the bed. As I entered the room he gave his cheerful grin and wink, but I was immediately aware that a change had taken place in him. What first prompted this feeling were his teeth. I had never noticed them before but they seemed more prominent than usual: his grin was wolfish. His face, never in any way chubby, had sharpened; flesh had collapsed onto the bones.

"Hello, son," he said. "What do you want?" The bonhomie was now no more than a facade, and I could smell something confused and resentful beneath. I did my dutiful best to wish him well and express the hope that he would be out of hospital and performing within a few days. As I did so his face remained blank, and he nodded sharply at each clumsy expression of good will. He seemed impatient. His hands fumbled with a piece of dark cloth. I asked him about the leg.

"It'll be fine," he said. "Just give us a few days. It'll mend. They're operating tonight. Don't you worry. That's a good leg. I'm not having it off in a hurry." I was puzzled: the possibility of amputation had not occurred to me. Syd's hands continued to work at the piece of cloth: he seemed to have taken on some of his wife's restlessness. When I told him that I now occupied his position in the skins he became animated.

"You don't want to do that, son," he said frowning.

I told him that I didn't want to do it, but I that was doing it under Bunny Goldman's orders. Syd did not take this in.

"Listen to me, lad," he said, drawing me closer to him with a beckoning finger. "She'll never work those skins without me. I tell you she's nothing without me. Nothing's going to change that. She can talk all she likes about Priscilla and *Mother Goose*. Oh, I know. It's Priscilla this, sodding Priscilla that. Well, she won't do no Priscilla. Understand? I'm seeing to that. Peggy and I do the skins together or we don't do it at all. All right, son?"

He bared his teeth again. The lustreless eyes were no longer on me but had concentrated themselves on a distant object. The skin was pale, tautly folded and shining. Something convulsed under his sheet and I left quickly.

~

I felt still more nervous about the evening performance. The atmosphere in the theatre had not improved. I gathered that Victor was not speaking to anyone, least of all Peggy. Quite why he had pursued an affair with her in the first place was beyond me. Maid Marian and Robin Hood's speculation was that it was wounded vanity: the star's *droit de seigneur* had been denied him in other quarters, so he had settled for the only available opportunity. Peggy alone was hurt by his aloofness because the rest of the company, in one of those periodic fits of self-righteousness that sometimes grip theatrical people, had decided to shun him as coldly as he shunned them.

Peggy herself had absorbed some of this mood of indignation and the object of her censure was still me and my alleged offence inside the skins that afternoon. I had stopped protesting my innocence. In her dressing room, I allowed her to give me a talking to and to heal her guilt with the balm of moral superiority.

"Whatever happens," she concluded. "I'm going solo in the skins after this. I'm going to ask Bunny to give me Priscilla next year, but I'll settle for Puss in Boots."

She was sitting at her dressing table as she said this and Dobbin's skins were lying at her feet, looking like the desiccated corpse of a farm animal. As she spoke the last words she must have kicked the skin accidentally; at least, I saw one of the cloth legs give a strange twitch like the last convulsion of a dying beast. Peggy noticed this too and seemed shocked. She put one of her stockinged feet carefully on Dobbin's head, then looked at me defiantly.

Long before the thing happened I was determined that this would be my last night in the skins. The stage lights beat down upon my mobile prison and made its darkness noisome and oppressive. I felt beads of sweat crawling off my bent back. The other occupant, so near yet so distant, was also in a state of agitation. How it was I don't know – perhaps it was my eyes – but the gauzes in the skin out of which I could see onto the stage had become more opaque. The events outside seemed dim and remote, and among the unpleasant odours which surrounded my captivity was a faint scent which oppressed me most of all, that of another person, not Peggy, but another.

It was our last entrance before the "Walk Down", the curtain call of the Pantomime. In this scene the Sheriff of Nottingham's villainy was finally exposed, and Dobbin had to come on to nudge him off to prison. We were waiting for our entrance in the wings when I felt something pass across my face, something yielding, cold and damp, like a cloth. It filled me with terror because it had no explanation and it left behind an intense version of that alien smell which so revolted me.

I heard Peggy's muffled voice urging me to "Get a move on! We're missing our entrance." So we trundled on, I now in a state of incommunicable panic. Then it happened again, just as Peggy had given the Sheriff of Nottingham the first butt with her head, rather more violently than usual as I remember. It was at that moment that I felt as if someone or something was trying to suffocate me. The cloth – if that was what it was – was being forced over my mouth and nose. I tried to bring my hands up to pull it off, but I was paralysed and somehow I dreaded touching the thing. Its odour was intense: it was yielding, a little slimy and somehow soft. It felt like someone's skin.

I was told later that having been violently sick inside the Pantomime Horse, I collapsed on stage. And the audience, seeing all this from the outside, roared with laughter.

That was my last night in the skins. I learned

later that Syd had died in the early hours of the following morning. Gangrene had set in and he stubbornly refused amputation. I had the impression from the nurse I spoke to that a loss of the will to live had played its part.

~

In the summer of 1981 Bunny G had nothing for me in the way of theatrical work because he had closed down the repertory side of his enterprise – it had never made much of a profit – and was concentrating on variety. But I was desperately hard up and out of work, so he took me on as a kind of office boy at their London Headquarters. I also became a roving trouble-shooter if there were stage management problems at any of his theatres. Bunny Goldman was one of those hard-faced businessmen who liked to think of themselves as having "a heart of gold" underneath it all. Everyone at the office repeated this mantra about Bunny's heart of gold, but I never saw enough of his heart to say what metal it was made of. Unless you count that blazingly hot August day when he came in and leaned over his secretary's desk.

"Millie, my love, I wonder if you can find a

nice bouquet of flowers for me." There was something in his tone of voice which announced to the world that he was about to make a gesture. "I've just heard some very sad news about Peggy Brinton."

He turned to me. "You remember Peggy, don't you?"

I nodded.

"Lovely lady. Real Pro. One of the old school. A trouper. Salt of the Earth." Moved by his own eloquence, he wiped something from his eye, then mopped his huge sweating head. He sighed. By this time he had commanded the attention of the whole office.

"I fear she is not long for this world." A pause, then he announced solemnly: "The big C." After which he nodded several times in a thoughtful way, as if he had personally given the diagnosis. Everyone in the office began to make aggrieved and sympathetic noises.

"I want a nice bouquet of flowers," he said, handing me a ten pound note. "Nothing fancy. Just a nice bouquet of flowers. And I would like you, my friend" – putting his hand on my shoulder – "to take it round to Peggy, personally, from me and all of us here. I have a card here which we can all sign." He produced a large specimen decorated with yellow roses. He had already signed the card with an enormous flourish and our little messages were to adorn the empty spaces around this central signature. After we had put our names to the gesture, he told me where to go. Peggy had recently come out of hospital and rather than returning to her house in Southend, she was being looked after by her son Mick at his flat near the Elephant and Castle.

That day London rippled in white, airless heat. Having bought the flowers – and even in 1981 a decent bouquet cost more than £10 – I made my way to Mick's flat. It was on the fifth floor of a huge block on the Old Kent Road. The lift had failed and the walk up a baking concrete stairwell was an exhausting, despairing journey. I think the heat blacked out some of my conscious memory because I remember suddenly and unexpectedly finding myself in front of a red door, one of many which opened onto a narrow balconied walkway. Down below traffic roared, houses hazed and shivered in the heat. I had a chance to recover my senses because a long time elapsed between my ringing the bell and the door being opened.

Standing in the doorway was a very large man in his thirties with a great senseless slab of a face. His huge bulk was clad in shorts and a black sweatshirt with LONDON PALLADIUM emblazoned on it in white.

"Hello," I said proffering a hand. "You must be Mick."

Mick looked at the hand, but did not move. He said: "Have you come to see Mum?" He pronounced the last word "Moom" which, in his cavernous, colourless voice had a suggestion of threat to it.

I nodded, showed him the flowers and explained their origin. Mick stared blankly at them and retreated an inch or two inside the doorway. I could see a narrow passage beyond and an open door to the right through which I could just discern a small, sweltering sitting room. There was a smell of unemptied kitchen bins and fried food.

"Moom don't like company no more." he said eventually.

"Will you give her these, then?" I said handing him the flowers. He hesitated warily before accepting them and withdrew a little further into the hot darkness of the passage.

Mick's great bulk made it impossible for me to pass him, but I could now see a little more of the sitting room. It was lit by the sun made pallid and bland by the yellow muslin curtains through which it filtered. The room was crammed with photographs and ornaments. Someone had decided to collect gaudy little china figurines of animals. In the midst of this in an armchair sat Peggy, her face white and shrivelled, the air and blood sucked out of her. She was smoking hard. From time to time she gave a convulsive twitch as if she were trying to shake off the loose robe of flesh which still clung to her bones. It was hot, horribly hot and stuffy, but she seemed to be wearing a sort of white woolly jump suit. I noticed that where she ought to have had shoes there were great orange webbed feet.

She saw me and opened her mouth, but no sound came out.

"Moom won't move out of the skins now," said Mick.

On the thirteenth of July last year, Dr. George Vilier, died suddenly at the age of fifty five. He was lecturer in Theatre Studies at Bath University, and a colleague and friend of mine, so I suppose it should have been no surprise to discover that he had made me his literary executor. Among his papers I found the almost complete MS of his long-awaited work, The Gothic Experience in Victorian Drama, which I hope will soon see publication. I also found a folder which contained the following documents and notes. I am sure that Vilier was intending to use them to form a single connected narrative, and I debated whether I should do the same. In the end I decided that I would serve his memory better if I arranged these papers in a moderately coherent order, secured the relevant copyright permissions and published them as they stood. I have added a short note at the end, but readers *must decide for themselves whether what follows provides any clue to the mystery of his sudden and tragic death.*

R.O. 2007

A collection of documents relating to the history of the Grand Pavilion Theatre, Seabourne compiled and annotated by the late George Vilier.

From *Britain on $50 a Day*

(Roughrider Press 2006)

Seabourne, Kent,
17 miles West of Folkestone, A259

Typical, old fashioned British South Coast resort, neat enough but lacking the character of Brighton. Quite attractive Victorian sea front worth a look: pier, bandstand etc. Some of the old hotels will do some very cheap weekend or midweek breaks out of season. Elegant Regency terraced houses in the town have been much knocked about and altered. The 18th Century Classical Revival church of St Thomas, built 1787, is an early work of the architect John Nash[i] and has an altarpiece depicting the Resurrection by the U.S. born Benjamin West.[ii] Boasts a really great old theater, the Grand Pavilion built 1893 and designed by the theater architect Frank Matcham.[iii] The imposing front is to be seen in King George Street but has been out of use since 1974 and in a truly shameful state of disrepair. (Theater freaks can visit interior on application to the Town Council Offices.)

~

From *Seabourne, a Brief Guide*

(Heritage Guides 1999)

Grand Pavilion Theatre, King George Street (Grade 2 listed building, visit by application only)

The Grand Pavilion has been described as a 'classic Matcham theatre'. It was completed in 1893 at the beginning of Matcham's great period of theatre building, and opened on March 28th of that year with a production of Lancelot Jones's society comedy *Lady Polly*. The exterior, now somewhat dilapidated, is well proportioned and the theatre perhaps derives its name from the pavilion-like structure that adorns the central tower. However, as with most Matcham theatres, it is the interior where his true genius is displayed. The decoration of the auditorium is lavish and done in an eclectic "Indian Baroque" style. The theatre boasted a number of innovations. Besides Matcham's much vaunted ventilation system, the stage machinery was unusually elaborate and designed to accommodate considerable spectacles. There are mobile and revolving stages which would allow chases, even horse races to take place, the horses galloping over an ever moving stage (operated by hydraulic machinery from beneath) with a mobile backdrop behind, thus giving an almost cinematic illusion of motion. Unfortunately during a performance of the famous horse racing melodrama *The Whip* in 1910 the machinery failed, a horse lost its footing and was hurled with its jockey into the orchestra pit. The rider was killed instantly and the horse sustained injuries so severe that it had to be put down. After this tragedy the machinery was never used again. Nevertheless the theatre remained, in theatrical parlance, a "number one touring date" and saw some notable productions, featuring the leading actors of the time, including the great Henry Irving in *The Corsican Brothers* and *The Bells,*[iv] and Sir John Martin Harvey in *The Only Way.*

In the twenties the theatre was visited by, among others, Sir Gerald Du Maurier, Jack Buchanan, and the Aldwych Farce team. It is rumoured that Fred and Adele Astaire once performed there in *Funny Face* in a so-called "flying matinee" (in which an entire London production would be transported from London for an afternoon). In the 1930s it became a repertory theatre and enjoyed mixed fortunes until the war when it became a concert venue for ENSA tours serving the nearby air force bases and the Seabourne Downs military camp. It was hit twice by incendiary bombs but sustained only minor damage.

In 1945 it was bought by the millionaire philanthropist, Kenneth Marlesford, mainly, it is thought, for the benefit of his actress wife, Jane Selway. There she played leading roles in some distinguished revivals of classics and West End plays. (Her Hedda Gabler is still remembered in the town.) In 1953, following another tragic accident in the theatre,

Marlesford sold the Grand Pavilion to Billy Cohen, and it became part of the Cohen-Majestic chain of theatres, specialising in variety and pantomime. Many of the leading variety stars of the time topped the bill here, including Bruce Forsyth, Frankie Laine, Max Miller (in one of his last appearances) and the singer Rex Raymond not long before a tragic car accident cut short his brilliant career. In 1966 when "live" variety was beginning to suffer from the competition of Television, Cohen-Majestic sold the theatre to the Seabourne Town Council for an undisclosed sum. It was then run for some years as a seasonal repertory theatre with a pantomime at Christmas, but with no great success. Companies came and went with disconcerting rapidity – no less than three in the Summer Season of 1972. Finally, in 1974 the Town Council closed the theatre down. Despite numerous public-spirited efforts to put it back to its original use the theatre remains derelict, though the Town Council, to its credit, has turned down applications to turn it into a Bingo Hall and a multiplex cinema.

~

From *Frank Matcham's Theatres* by Oliver Osborne-Pritchard F.R.I.B.A.

(Vitruvius Books 1984)

Grand Pavilion Theatre, Seabourne

"See here the Bourne of lovers of the Muse
Whose temple Seabourne's citizens may use.
And now on stage we'll strive to play our part
To match the skill of Matcham's matchless art."

So ran the last lines of the "dedicatory ode" which opened the Grand Pavilion Theatre on March 28th 1893. It was spoken in front of the curtain before the first performance by no less a person than Ellen Terry.[v] Sadly laboured though the verses are, they do demonstrate how highly the theatre's architect was rated. How different from fifty or so years later when Matcham theatres were being destroyed wholesale to make way for uglier, cheaper and more transitory buildings which met their own fate in a much shorter period of time. Fortunately for the Grand Pavilion, by the time it closed its doors as a theatre, Frank Matcham was beginning to be appreciated again and a preservation order on the theatre was already in place.

Nevertheless it is now in a sorry state. An air of general neglect, indeed total surrender to the forces of decay, pervades. The roof of the dressing rooms on the top floor has caved in; there is wood rot in all parts of the building and a deep pool of black, oily water can be seen (and smelt) in the orchestra pit where the permanent pumping system put in by Matcham has completely failed. As a result I was unable to examine the elaborate machinery installed beneath the stage. The unusually high fly tower is now a tangle of ropes with forgotten backdrops and cut-out flats of trees and rocks hanging at crazy angles, so that too is hard to appraise.

I was able to obtain access through the good offices of the caretaker and former stage doorman Mr Jack Pegley. Mr. Pegley, something of a character, insisted that the proper designation of his role was "hallkeeper", an old fashioned term. He was obviously proud of "his" theatre, though saddened by its present state of dilapidation, and curiously reluctant to show me certain parts of his domain.

In spite of the decay it is still plain to see that

the interior is an early Matcham masterwork. Indian motifs pervade throughout in the auditorium and foyers. The main ceiling is encrusted with fine rococo plaster scrollwork which frames cartouches on which Indian scenes have been painted: dancing nautch girls, a durbar, a tiger hunt, and, rather curiously, a scene of suttee in which an Indian widow is shown burning on the pyre of her dead husband. I had the opportunity to inspect this last at close quarters and can testify to the strange vividness with which the unknown artist has depicted a look of agony and despair, clearly visible though the flames and smoke, on the face of the young widow. I am quite sure however that very few visitors to the theatre would have given a second glance at this rather macabre insight into Indian life: the cartouche in question is only visible from the cheaper seats in the Gallery.

Indian arches support the ceiling from columns, the capitals of which are in the form of double elephants' heads facing the stage and the back wall. The effect of these is ponderous and perhaps a little sinister, but impressive. The boxes are made to look like howdahs or pavilions fit for a Maharajah.

I was interested in these boxes particularly as I had discovered in my researches that one of them, the prompt side stage box, had, at the request of the original owner, been installed by Matcham with a speaking tube system by which means the box's occupant could be in contact with the stage manager in the prompt corner at stage level. This was only one of the many innovative features of the Grand Pavilion, but it is, as far as I know, the only one unique to this particular theatre. The first proprietor, The Hon. Arthur Faversham, a minor poet and keen amateur of the theatre, something of a dilettante by all accounts, is said to have kept the box permanently reserved for his personal use, and to have maintained communication with staff and even performers by means of this device. Records show, however, that debts and some aftershocks of the scandal surrounding Wilde, with whose circle Faversham was associated, forced him to flee abroad in 1896. (We also find his name mentioned in papers relating to the Cleveland Street Scandal of 1889.) I was anxious to discover whether the management which bought the theatre from Faversham, Joel Abernethy Theatres Ltd, or subsequent owners had continued to make use of this facility.

My anxiety to inspect the box was not, for reasons unexplained, matched by Mr Pegley's eagerness to show it to me. Though he had been helpful in other respects, he point blank refused to enter the box and left me to do so by myself. I only mention this because it is indicative of the curious atmospheric hold this theatre has on people – even, I must admit, myself.

I discovered the communication system in the box almost immediately. It is situated behind a red velvet curtain about two foot square which covers a small alcove in the wall that adjoins the proscenium arch. Not only had the system remained in use but, around the late nineteen forties or early fifties I should guess, it had been replaced by an electric Tannoy system complete with microphone, speaker and volume control knob. I casually switched on the speaker's knob and, to my surprise, the thing appeared to be still operational. (Pegley had turned on the electrics for my benefit.) A barrage of static was followed by a strange whistling or whispering sound that resembled human voices. I called out to Pegley to see if he had gone down to the stage level, but he had not.

I did not stay long in the box because I found myself subjected to a curiously strong draught of cold air. I could not quite locate its source. Obviously something connected with Matcham's famous "air duct" ventilation system had gone badly wrong; hardly surprising after ten or so years of sustained neglect.

~

From *Journal of Paranormal Research* Vol X No. 9
(July 1975)

"The Grand Pavilion, Seabourne: a Haunted Theatre?"
by Harrison Bews

Investigations were prompted by reports coming in about the theatre from various quarters beginning in 1972, including one detailed account from the actor Rodney D. Some scepticism was expressed about this testimony as Rodney D had described himself at various times to our researchers as a "psychic" and "clairvoyant", but his account, part of which we will come to later, was given in a relatively level-headed manner. Moreover it was corroborated at various crucial points by a number of other witnesses. However, general murmurs about the Grand Pavilion being a "jinxed theatre" may be safely disregarded as the loose talk of a profession which by its very nature is unusually prone to superstition.

Phenomena experienced were concentrated in two main areas, though a number of witnesses testify to sudden feelings of disquiet, sensations of cold, the feeling of being watched etc. in other parts of the theatre.

The first main centre of psychic disturbance – henceforward referred to as Location (Loc.) A – was the stage area and the wings on what is known as "the prompt side", i.e. the right hand side of the stage as the spectator views it. This is where the prompter (usually the chief stage manager) sits with the "book" or script, and directs his assistants in any change of scenery or lighting. Many actors had testified to a sense of being pushed, or somehow psychically impelled, to the edge of the stage, so that there was a danger of falling into the orchestra pit which is unusually deep and cavernous. Almost a third of those questioned on the subject say that this unpleasant sensation was accompanied by the sound, low and almost imperceptible, of growling, "like the growling of a dog." Some also heard a breathy panting, again like that of a dog. One person only thought he heard the whinnying of a horse.

The other sound most frequently heard in Loc. A was that of tapping. All those questioned about this were quite specific about the nature of this tapping and that it was altogether different to the usual sounds made by a theatre with antiquated heating systems, wooden structures in varying stages of decay etc. The sound seemed to all of them to be like that of a stick, perhaps a light walking stick, being tapped on the floor. Commonly the subject would hear the tapping while engaged upon some task in Loc. A, but when he or she turned their full attention upon the noise it would cease. This could be experienced a number of times in succession. Thus the subject would turn back to the task in hand and the tapping would begin again; the subject would stop whatever he or she was doing and listen, the tapping would stop, then begin again when the subject stopped listening for it, and so on.

The second centre of psychic phenomena (henceforward referred to as Loc. B) was the prompt side stage box, i.e. the box to be found nearest to the stage on the prompt side. It may as well be stated that much superstition surrounds this box, which is known for reasons which we were unable to discover as "The Blind Man's Box." It was hardly ever occupied and tickets would only be sold for it in the rare event of a "full house".

Many of the phenomena surrounding Loc. B have been in fact witnessed from Loc. A. A number of witnesses testify to having been on stage (in several instances during a performance) and having seen a shadowy figure watching from it when it was known that no-one could possibly have been in the box. The figure has no features but is often said to have "eyes", that is two points of pale light are seen emanating from the shadowy presence where eyes might reasonably be supposed to be. The clearest account of this unusual manifestation is to be found in the testimony of the aforementioned Rodney D, a twenty five year old actor. His account, recorded by one of our researchers, dates from the year 1973:

"It was changeover day and we were changing the set for a new production. We were clearing *Dial M for Murder* and were setting up for *How the Other Half Loves*. As you can only begin the changeover after the end of a performance these things can go on late into the night. This one was a bugger. As you know, *How the Other Half Loves* has this weird double location set and we were having trouble working it all out. Anyway, round about midnight we decided to down tools for a coffee. We were done in. I was sitting on the edge of the stage, in the dead middle where the stage bows out a little into the auditorium, with my legs dangling in the pit. I had a brew in one hand and a ciggy in the other – murder for the old voice box, I know. Anyway, you know how you suddenly get this urge to look in a certain direction – well, I do – and I felt myself almost forced to look up to my left, to the prompt side stage box. For a couple of moments I resisted; then I thought, what the hell. There was something in the box. If you're in any way psychic like I am you'll know what I mean: it was more a presence than an actual visual thing, but I did see something. It was the shape of a man, a sort of shadow almost dead black, and he was leaning forward, his head almost over the edge of the box. He was not sideways on, profile; he was facing towards me with his right ear towards the stage, and it was as if he were listening, hard. And I saw what I suppose were eyes, only they were very pale and sort of luminous. In spite of the eyes I felt sure he couldn't see me, but I think he could hear me. I'm sure he could because when I coughed and dropped my ciggy into the pit he started and turned his head round, and it was as if he was turning his head to hear where I was. My God, it was horrible. I don't know why but it was. I called to the others who were lounging about in the Prompt Corner. I said there was someone in the Blind Man's Box. No, I've no idea why it's called that, nor does anyone. At least – Anyway, they all came trooping onto the stage and of course they couldn't see anything in the box and, to tell the truth, by that time neither could I. And that was it really, except – oh! – just as this thing was turning its head I bloody nearly fell into the pit."

This is the clearest account of what was seen

in Loc. B, though one detail is supplied by another witness, the stage designer Adrian C. He claims to have seen the figure on a number of occasions. His description is vaguer than that of Rodney D in all respects but one. In describing the "eyes", he said they were luminous and described them as being of "a pale, bluey, greeny, milky colour, like light shining through Lalique glass."

A strong reluctance to enter Loc. B was felt by many witnesses, though some claim to have tried to investigate and found it unaccountably locked. The few who did enter did not stay long, finding it suddenly prone to blasts of chill air and, as one witness rather cryptically put it, "full of little noises."

The person who had worked in the theatre for the longest time, the "hallkeeper" a Mr Jack P, was questioned on a number of occasions but was either unable or unwilling to supply any relevant information about the theatre and its history.

Investigators were allowed in, shortly after the theatre had closed down, in 1975, but encountered nothing out of the ordinary during the daytime. During our one and only all-night session – the Council, for some unknown reason permitted us to set up our equipment for one night only – some tapping of the kind described by a number of witnesses was heard and recorded, but this could be put down to the usual odd noises to which a large building in a very poor state of repair is prone. One of our researchers was loitering along the front of the stage when she distinctly felt a hand in the small of her back impelling her towards the orchestra pit. This only occurred once and no other investigator enjoyed this sensation so it may be put down as a questionable phenomenon. Much of the research naturally centred round Loc. B where the main body of psychic activity had been observed in the initial reports. It has to be said that very little of a definitely paranormal nature was observed. On two occasions our equipment recorded significant localised drops in temperature within the box, but this could be ascribed to the draughts which pervaded the theatre. On several occasions in daylight and during the night, investigators (myself included) felt a sudden blast of cold air on the back of the neck, but again natural causes for these cannot be entirely excluded. One event may be noteworthy and it occurred to me. At about two o'clock in the morning I was examining the equipment which had been installed in the box for communicating with the Prompt corner at the side of the stage. I was endeavouring to determine whether this could be the source of the sudden localised falls in temperature which had been recorded. Suddenly I began to hear noises coming through the speaker which relayed messages from the prompt corner. They sounded like whispering, urgent and furtive, though I could distinguish no words. There appeared to be two voices, possibly a man's and a woman's. It was curious because I had taken care to check that the speaker was turned off when I began my session in the stage box. I checked again and found that the speaker was off. I switched the knob on and off several times but this appeared to make no difference. The sounds continued intermittently for several minutes and then faded altogether. I later ascertained that during the time when this phenomenon occurred none of our researchers had been anywhere near either Loc. A or Loc. B.

~

From: *The Daily Telegraph*
November 30th 1971, Obituaries page

Sir Kenneth Marlesford C.B.E., *Industrialist and Philanthropist known as "The Blind Billionaire"* **(1885-1971)**

Sir Kenneth Marlesford who died at the age of 86 was one of the last of the old school of great industrial magnates. Born in the palmy days of the British Empire, he represented the sturdy values of that era, its overwhelming sense of patriotic duty, and also, perhaps, a certain inflexibility in the unquestioning conviction of the justice of its own cause. As an arms manufacturer he played a key role in both world wars, a role which made him powerful, influential and phenomenally rich. The sobriquet "The Blind Billionaire" may well have been first coined by the press with alliteration rather than accuracy in mind, but it probably reflects the state of his finances towards the end of his long life. He was born in Salford in 1885, the son of Ezekiel Marlesford, a manufacturer of moderately priced sporting guns. Kenneth Marlesford is said to have been to the Manchester Grammar School, though there is no record of his attendance there. Certainly he began working for his father's firm, the Marlesford Gun Company, at a comparatively early age and was very soon demonstrating remarkable energy and business acumen. By the time he was in his twenties he had, due to his own abilities and his father's ailing health, taken over the direction of the firm which in 1911 became the Marlesford Light Arms Company. By this time the firm had already secured contracts to supply the military with small arms and light field artillery. With the advent of the First World War came a further expansion and another change of name to Imperial Armaments Ltd. It was the war that made Marlesford a millionaire, but the advent of peace saw no dwindling of the business. The subsequent expansion of Imperial Armaments throughout the 20s and 30s was at the expense of other firms, many of which Marlesford took over or bought up, employing business tactics that are more familiar today than they were then. It was in 1935 however that he suffered his first setback, though this was more on a personal than a business level. Accounts of how he was blinded differ, but on certain facts there is general agreement. There had been some unrest at one of his factories in Sunderland owing to the lack of safety precautions provided for the men who were working on the manufacture of a new kind of incendiary shell. Marlesford went in person to investigate the cause of unease and settle the dispute. It while he was inspecting arrangements that the accident occurred: there was an explosion and he received the full force of some virulent chemical compound in his eyes. Rumours that the event was not accidental, but the deliberate contrivance of disaffected workers, have persisted; however, nothing was ever proved. Within the year the Sunderland plant closed down resulting in many people being thrown out of work. Marlesford did not let his blindness affect his energies and ambitions, and the fact that he remained in full command of a powerful and ever-expanding industrial concern in spite of his visual impairment is testimony to a character of extraordinary tenacity and fortitude. During the Second World War his position as one of Britain's key arms manufacturers secured him a place in the secret councils of the war office, and he formed close alliances with Lord Beaverbrook (Minister for Procurement) and others of Churchill's inner circle. Despite his handicap he had the ear of Churchill himself who referred to him in private, affectionately enough it is thought, as "Blind Pew". In 1943 he married a 26 year old actress, Jane Selway, to the surprise of many who thought him a confirmed bachelor, but the couple appeared, in the early years of their marriage at least, to be devoted, and he did much to promote his wife's theatrical career. The differing climate of the post-war years brought changes in the industry, but no diminution of Marlesford's energies. In recognition of Britain's new role in the world, Marlesford changed the name of his firm again from Imperial Armaments to Advance Systems International. After the tragic suicide in 1953 of his wife, Marlesford became something of a recluse and put his business concerns in the hands of a management consortium of which he remained chairman until his death. Notwithstanding this withdrawal from the world, he began to give generously to various charitable and political causes, and it was these numerous benefactions which earned him a knighthood in 1967. (He had been awarded the C.B.E in 1945 for his wartime services.) He had no children and has left the bulk of his fortune to the Actor's Benevolent Fund.

~

From: *The Seabourne Mercury*
Monday August 18th 1952

ACTOR IN TRAGIC DEATH FALL
Horrific Discovery by Stage Doorman

At some time during the night of August 16th or the early hours of the 17th a tragedy occurred at the Grand Pavilion Theatre, Seabourne which has police baffled. On the morning of August 17th Mr Jack Pegley, stage doorman and caretaker of the Grand Pavilion, had opened up the theatre and was doing his customary round of inspection when he noticed that something was amiss in the orchestra pit. There he discovered to his horror the body of a man who had evidently fallen from the stage into the pit and broken his neck, though precisely how or why remains a mystery.

The body was quickly identified as that of actor, Roland Payne (31) who only the night before had been appearing at the theatre as "Bruce Lovell" opposite Jane Selway in a revival of Frank Vosper's tense drama *Love From a Stranger*. Mr Payne, a popular figure both in the town and among his colleagues, had been playing leading roles at the theatre this summer, and had scored notable successes as Gregory Black in *The Late Edwina Black* and Thomas Mendip in *The Lady's Not For Burning*.

Whether foul play was involved or whether this was simply a tragic accident, police are unable to say at this moment, but the case has certain puzzling features. Mr. Pegley has told the police that the theatre, to the best of his knowledge, was empty when he locked the stage door the previous night, and that it was still locked when he opened it the following morning.

Police investigations continue. Leading actress Jane Selway and her husband, the owner of the theatre, Mr. Kenneth Marlesford, are said to be deeply shocked and distressed by the event.

~

From: *The Diary and Notebook of George Vilier.*

Friday July 6th 2007

Train to Seabourne this afternoon. The town seemed to be full, but fortunately I had booked into "Sunnydene Guest House" on the front for the week.

I'd better state why I'm here, and why I have begun to keep this journal. I had been interested in "the Seabourne Tragedy", as it was known in our family, for a long time because Roland Payne was my Uncle. As I was a month old when he died I never met him, and it was only recently that I had the leisure to investigate the case. My parents also died when I was comparatively young and were, in any case, reticent about the affair. The above clipping from *The Seabourne Mercury* found in a drawer was all I had to go on.

Monday July 9th 2007

Until today I have found very few people who knew anything about the events of August 1952, let alone remembered them personally. It was quite by luck that I was put in touch with someone who was able to help me. Something had gone wrong with the exhaust of my Renault and, on enquiring after repair garages in the area with Renault dealerships, I was recommended Pegley's Garage on the Folkestone Road. Of course, the name Pegley was familiar to me from the press cutting about my uncle. It turned out that the proprietor, Tom Pegley, was the son of Jack Pegley who had died in 1991 aged 85.

Tom Pegley is a friendly man. He was intrigued by my interest but could tell me nothing of relevance beyond the fact that his father, despite having been little more than a humble theatre caretaker, died a comparatively wealthy man. But, he said, there was a box of papers and other items belonging to his father, which he had never troubled to look through. Would I care to see them?

The lack of curiosity that some people have about themselves and their origins always surprises, even shocks me, but I was glad to be allowed an uncensored look at this virgin material. Among the miscellaneous memorabilia of a life spent in theatrical environs there was one item which looked promising. It was a large brown manilla envelope containing something flat and cylindrical. The flap had been secured with sealing wax, and on it was written words to the effect that it was only to be opened on Pegley's death, except on his express instructions. Tom told me that it had been sent to him on his father's death by a firm of Seabourne solicitors who had been keeping it for him. No, he had never thought of opening it. No, he didn't mind if I did.

The envelope contained another envelope, typewritten and addressed to "Mr J. Pegley" which had been carefully resealed. By the feel of it it contained a letter. Then there was the flat cylindrical object which I had felt. It was a reel of audio tape, eight or nine inches in diameter, of the kind which could be played on those big old-fashioned "reel to reel" tape recorders of the 50s and 60s.

As it happened, Tom said, he still had the old Grundig tape recorder which his father had salvaged from the theatre when it closed. We played a few seconds of the tape and when Tom heard that it was his father's voice on it he stopped the machine. He does not want to listen to his dead father's voice. I suppose I can understand that. Tom has given me the tape and the recorder to take back to my guest house. I am going to transcribe what his father says and give him a copy.

Tuesday July 10th 2007
I have been sitting up all night listening with earphones on, transcribing Jack Pegley's tape. I have hardly had time to think about what he said, and perhaps that is just as well. I give it here complete without any expurgations.

"Testing... Can you hear me? Right. This is Jack Pegley. I am Jack Pegley and I wish to state... I am the Hallkeeper of the Grand Pavilion theatre. That's right, hallkeeper. None of this caretaker, stage doorman rubbish. I been with the Grand Pavilion a long time. Before the war I started. Stage Carpenter, I was then, when there was stage carpenters. I was a flyman too; did all sorts. That was before Mr Marlesford, Sir Kenneth as he became, bought the theatre. I was there before him. Then when I injured my knee down that orchestra pit, they made me hallkeeper and I ran the corner. The Prompt Corner to you. I was in charge. Well, Mr Marlesford, he trusted me. He said I was his eyes. Blind he was, Mr Marlesford. "Pegley," he said, "be my eyes." So I was. Now this what I'm saying is for a reason, so I'm not telling any funny stories, only what I got to. [*A pause. Pegley seems to be breathing hard.*] Right then. Mrs Marlesford, she was Jane Selway, the leading lady and what she said went in the theatre. Mr Marlesford, he allowed that, and anyway he had his own, the arms and that, but he come down every weekend and sometimes in the week and he sits in the box with his guide dog Wisper, and he listens to the show, and sometimes he talks to me through the Tannoy we had made for him in his box where the old speaking tubes used to be. "Pegley, are you there?" he says, whispering to me through the machine to me in the prompt corner. "Pegley, are you there?" And I says, "yes, sir, Mr Marlesford and it's five minutes to the end of act one," or some such. And he says: "Pegley, leave the mike on so's I can hear you in the prompt corner," so I do that. He likes to hear me give my orders to ring down the curtain or dim the straws in the battens, or some such. Well Jane Selway, I call her Jane, because she says: "Call me Jane. Everyone calls me Jane," she's a fine, beautiful young woman and a fine actress. I see her do all sorts. "You should have seen her," I says once to Mr Marlesford, accidental, and he says "I can't!" All sharp and sudden like. He had a cold temper on him sometimes. Well, here's the thing. Jane, she gets on with everyone, but specially with this young man who comes down from London. Roland Payne, his name was. Comes down having been in one of Mr Binkie Beaumont's shows at the Haymarket. Oh, it's Binkie this and Binkie that, and dear Noel and darling Boo Laye and what not, but he could act a bit, I'll say that. Well, he and Jane they get on famously and that season, 1952 it was, I'll never forget, they're a team, like leading man and leading lady. Roland Payne and Jane Selway. They get a bit of a following, and people want to come and see Payne and Selway. Most nights they're selling out, and it's a big house, I tell you, thousand seater plus. Well, one night, it's *Love from a Stranger* – no, I tell a lie, that came later: it's *The Lady's Not For Burning*. I remember there was a lot of fancy talk in that show. Well, I was in the prompt corner during Act I and I hear Mr Marlesford on the Tannoy "Pegley, are you there?" He says. And I say, "yes, sir, Mr Marlesford; it's twenty minutes to the Act

One curtain, and I'm just nipping round to the Opposite Prompt side to put another stage weight on one of the braces. There's a flat flapping about horrible. I've got plenty of time and they won't need me on the book, so I'd rather see to it myself." And he says: "Right you are, Pegley, but still leave the mike on so's I can hear the prompt corner." So that's what I do and then I went round to the OP and I fix the stage weight. And as I do so I look across the stage and see Roland and Jane in the wings on the other side, waiting to go on. They're standing by my desk and talking, and touching, and I wonder if they know my microphone's on. Well, it's only a thought and I forget it when I get back to the prompt corner. Then it's getting ready to bring the curtain down on act one. And it's a big line from Mr Roland Payne that rings down the curtain: "For God's sake hang me, before I love that woman!" I remember that. Funny stuff. The curtain drops, big round of applause and we bring in the iron for the interval. Then I hear on the Tannoy: "Pegley, are you there?" It's Mr. Marlesford in his box. It was a shock like because I'd forgotten him. So I says, "yes, sir, Mr Marlesford. I'm here." And he says: "Did you see them?" Just that. It took me a time to figure it out what he meant and then the penny drops. So I says, "yes, sir, Mr Marlesford. I did see." Then he just says: "We know," and clicks off. Well, I'm sticking to what's important now, but let's just say as the weeks pass it's plain what's going on. Mr Marlesford, he says nothing, but when he's in his box he always tells me to keep my mike on, and sometimes he sends me off if I'm not busy in the corner to check the box office returns, or some such, just to get me away from the corner. I know what he's up to. Anyway, we start on a two week run of *Love from a Stranger*. Always goes down well, that show; and Jane is playing the girl, and Mr Payne he's playing the villain, Bruce, and we come to the Saturday, end of the first week. Mr Marlesford he's come down to see the Saturday night show, but I don't hear from him down the Tannoy till right at the end just before the curtain: "Pegley, are you there?" he says. So I says, "yes, sir, Mr Marlesford. I'm here." And he says: "Come up and see me in the box after the show." Well, that's a turn up for a start. He's never done that before, so up I go after the show. And there he is bolt upright in his chair with his black guide dog Wisper lying flat on the carpet underneath it. "Pegley," he says, "I want you to do something for me. Nodder" – that's his chauffeur – "will drive my wife and self back to the Seabourne house, then he's taking me to London. Now then, where does Mr Payne go for a drink after the show?" I says it's usually The Feathers. "Right then," he says. "When you leave the theatre tonight, I want you to throw the main electricity switch in the prompt corner like you always do, but I don't want you to lock up as per, I want you to leave the stage door unlocked. Do you understand?" I says yes. He says: "Then you take your time, but you go over to The Feathers and you find Mr Roland Payne and you say to him these words: 'There's someone waiting for you on stage at the theatre. Go now. The stage door's unlocked.' Just that. Then you skedaddle." And it's as if he can see me opening my mouth to say something, because the next thing he says is. "Don't ask any questions. I'll see the stage door is locked afterwards, and I'll see you don't lose by it. That's all." Then he gets up and picks up his stick and whistles to Wisper who leads him out of the box and through the pass door and down to his wife's dressing room. And I'm left standing there in the box, scratching my head and not knowing what to think. Well, I do exactly what I'm told and I go to The Feathers and I give Mr. Payne the message. And there's one funny thing. When I give him what I'm told to say, Mr. Payne he doesn't seem surprised. He just nods his head and gives a little smile, like what they call a smirk, and then he looks at me like he wants me to get out of there, so I do. And then the more I think about it, the more I don't like it. It's not that I can put my finger on it, but it smells nasty. So I wait round the corner from The Feathers – it's a fine night with a big moon – and not long after I see Mr Payne come out of The Feathers with his trilby on cocked at an angle, cheeky like, and he hurries towards the Grand Pav. Well, I follow at a distance because I know where he's going, and I go round the theatre the other way so I won't be seen by him. And that's where I see round the side, in the shadow of the theatre made by the moon, there's a car. It's Mr Marlesford's Rolls with Nodder in his uniform standing beside it. Now that gets me really worried, I don't know why, but it does, so I hurry round to the stage door and Mr Payne, he must already have gone in, so I go in. Almost the first thing I hear when

I'm in is this sort of crash and coming from the stage, it sounds like. Well, like a fool, I try to switch on a light and I've forgotten that I threw the mains switch to the building at the prompt corner. Still, I should know my way by now, so I feel hand over hand along the wall to one of the pass doors onto the stage. By God, it's black as the ace of spades in there. I can't see a thing, but I can hear. My Christ, I can hear. It's someone screaming out in agony, like you can feel the pain yourself. It's coming from somewhere near the stage, but there's an echo, hollow like. And it goes on, this screaming. It's Mr Payne, I know the voice, and now I've worked out where he is. He's in the orchestra pit because it's deep and hollow. I feel my way round the back wall and then the prompt side wall towards the corner, and all the time there's this screaming going on. But now it's getting weaker and mixed up in it is a sort of coughing and what I call a gurgle, like he's choking on jam or something thick and sticky. Now I've got to the prompt corner and I stop dead still. Then there's this great big choke and it stops. Everything's quiet for a second – silence – and I'm just reaching up to where I think the mains switch is going to be when I hear this other sound. It's like tap, tap, tap of a stick on the stage and the patter of paws and the breath of a dog. It's coming my way towards the prompt corner but I can't see a thing. Everything's as black as bloody hell. He's coming closer. I hold my breath. I say nothing. He's three, four feet away and I can almost smell him. Wisper gives a little low growl, like she does, and he says: "Pegley, are you there?" I say nothing, and again he says "Pegley, are you there?" That's when I run, bumping into him as I go and he's wearing this long overcoat of soft cashmere like, soft and cold. I don't know how, I find my way to the pass door and then I'm out of there. My wife, she lets me in three or four in the morning, and I'd got through a bottle of Bell's by then, so she thinks she knows the reason, except I'm not usually a big drinker. Later that morning I have to go back to the theatre, though I don't usually go in on a Sunday. Then a few days afterwards Mr Marlesford and I have a talk, and he says he'll see me all right. But I'm making sure he does, so when you hear this I might be dead; and if I'm dead and Mr Marlesford – Sir Kenneth, I should say – is still alive, then you know what to do."

When I had transcribed the tape, and read it over, I opened the letter that was with the tape. It was addressed to Mr. Pegley from a firm of London solicitors:

Parkins, Wraxall & Worby, Solicitors

1 Lupton Court

Gutter Lane

Cheapside

London E. C. 2.

Dec. 5th 1971

Dear Mr Pegley,

We have been instructed by the Estate of the late Sir Kenneth Marlesford and under the conditions of his will to charge you with the following task.

You are to come to these offices at the above address and collect from us the urn containing the late Sir Kenneth's ashes and take them by train to Seabourne. There you are to gain access to the Grand Pavilion Theatre and place or scatter those ashes "where," in the words of Sir Kenneth's List of Instructions signed and dated 23rd December 1970 "Mr. Pegley knows I wish them to be so placed or scattered."

For this task you are to receive the sum of

£500 plus expenses. Should you reveal the nature of this task, or any of the contents of this letter to any person whatsoever (family members included) you will at once forfeit the pension which Sir Kenneth has allowed that you should continue to be paid under the provisions of his last will and testament signed, dated and witnessed, 23rd December 1970.

We await your response at your earliest convenience,

Yours etc,

Sydney Wraxall

I asked Tom whether his father had fulfilled this obligation. Tom says he doesn't know, but he thinks he remembers his father going up to London (a thing he rarely if ever did) at about that time. "Anyway," said Tom, "our dad was never one to pass up the offer of a bit of extra cash."

I did not ask Tom precisely how his father had died, but, as it happens, he volunteered the information. It happened in November 1991. Pegley was alone in his house, his wife having died three years previously, and he was sleeping in the first floor bedroom. At some time in the early hours of the morning he got up, presumably to answer the call of nature. He switched on the passage light, but the bulb blew and fused all the lights. One can only speculate what happened next but it was probably in the confusion which followed this minor mishap that Mr Pegley took a step or two in the wrong direction and ended by falling down his own stairs and breaking his neck.

There had been an inquest, but the jury brought in a verdict of accidental death.

Wednesday July 11th 2007

Today I managed to gain access to the theatre and stayed there just long enough to testify that the interior is indeed a splendid example of Frank Matcham's art. I don't want to write anything further about my experiences in the Grand Pavilion, Seabourne, except this: my quest is over, but what I have found will remain with me...

~

This is where George Vilier's diary ended. A few days later his body was found at the bottom of Beachy Head some miles further down the coast. No indication can be found – apart perhaps from that ambiguous last sentence – that he was suffering from depression, or that his mind was unbalanced.

R.O. 2007

Notes:

[i] John Nash (1752-1835) designed the great "Nash Terraces" in London and the Royal Pavilion, Brighton etc. It is thought that the row of terraced houses in Seabourne's Courteney Street are by Nash. [G.V.]

[ii] Benjamin West (1738-1820) was born near Springfield Pennsylvania. He succeeded Joshua Reynolds as President of the Royal Academy and pioneered the art of "history painting" in this country. [G.V.]

[iii] Frank Matcham (1854-1920) was the greatest and most prolific of British Theatre architects. Between 1879 and 1912 he designed and built some 92 theatres, rebuilt 52 more, and was responsible for several more buildings with theatrical connections, such as the great Tower Ballroom, Blackpool. Only about 25 of his theatres still stand, some of these, like the Grand

Pavilion, Seabourne, in a sad state of disrepair. [G.V.]

iv Almost certainly wrong. There are no records of the great Henry Irving (1838-1905) visiting this theatre. The writer is confusing him with his son H. B. Irving who did visit the theatre on tour with revivals of his father's classic vehicles *The Corsican Brothers* and *The Bells* (a tale of supernatural revenge). [G.V.]

v Ellen Terry (later Dame Ellen) was at the time Henry Irving's leading lady. She had a cottage in nearby Winchelsea where she was enjoying an Easter break from work at the Lyceum at the time she fulfilled this engagement. (see Joy Melville, *Ellen and Eddy*, Pandora Press 1987. p. 146) [G.V.]

"She's very collectable, you know," said the stall holder.

"Elsie Grace? Can't say I've heard of her."

"Oh, yes. Big musical comedy star of the Edwardian Theatre. One of the most photographed women of her time. As they say, the camera loved her."

When you are on a theatre tour, time lies heavy on your hands in the middle of the day. You might meet your friends in the company for a coffee, or perhaps lunch; you try to do some sightseeing. That day, in Norwich, back in 1972, I had seen a poster for an "Antiques and Collector's Fair" in a church hall. I had suggested it as an attraction to some others in the company, but nobody seemed much interested, so I had gone by myself.

I had no intention of buying anything; I never do, but I sometimes succumb to temptation. On this occasion there was not much to interest me. Old topographical prints: no. Vintage vinyl jazz records: no. American horror comics in cellophane envelopes: no. Model railway accessories: oh, no. But then there was a stall packed with old postcards in transparent plastic sleeves, with a large section devoted to the theatre. This consisted mainly of postcard portraits, in black and white or sepia tones, of once famous actors and actresses, among whom the collectable Elsie Grace featured prominently.

For theatre people, such memorabilia offer pleasing moments of nostalgia for a time when employment on the stage was more regular and secure, but also some sad reflection on the transience of theatrical fame. Who was Elsie Grace? What happened to her? A star had faded from the firmament and the world was less bright because of it, but few had noticed its passing.

The face that confronted me in various demure but enticing poses was not quite the classic Edwardian beauty: those heavy, Venus de

Milo features that were so much admired; the well managed curls, the confident, soulful gaze were not present. Elsie, when not showing off her profile, was looking at you with coquettish mischief in her eyes. The features, regular if a little thin were, as the French say, *piquant*. One of the postcards, a full-length photo, delicately hand-tinted with pink and pistachio green, bore the legend:

ELSIE GRACE AS "MISS PHOEBE SUNBEAM" IN "THE PEPPERMINT GIRL"

There she was, head slightly lowered smiling up at you through her lashes and showing off her exquisite if well corseted figure. She was holding up her dress so that you could see, beneath a froth of white petticoat, her perfect legs up to the calf, sheathed in white silk stockings. One leg was thrust forward, in a dancer's pose, and the little feet were shod in gleaming white ballet pumps. That faded elegance and innocence had a charm for me that I could not fully explain. It reminded me, for some reason, of the lavender scented drawers in my grandmother's house where, as a very young boy, I first became conscious of a past that was not mine, but which, in some mysterious way, still lived.

That day I bought four postcards of Elsie Grace in different poses, including the one of her as "Miss Sunbeam". I was not sure what I would do with them. I had a vague idea of mounting the cards and putting them all in one frame as a set. I placed them in a desk drawer in my flat and forgot about them, for the time being.

The tour ended and I began to find myself perilously out of work. The savings I had made on tour dwindled rapidly and my agent had come up with nothing better than a few days on a commercial for shaving cream. I wanted some form of employment badly.

Then, in a pub, I met an actor friend called Max who was just about to start in a television series. After commiserating with my situation from the condescending heights of his own fast approaching prosperity, he mentioned that, thanks to his success, he was quitting a temporary job helping out at Kendall Hall, "a sort of Theatrical Old Folks Home", as he termed it, in Croydon. If I applied immediately to replace him, he said, he could "put in a good word" for me. I swallowed what pride I had left and accepted his offer.

"Most of them are several sandwiches short of a picnic, but it can be interesting," said Max. The long and the short of it was I got the job.

It is some fifty years now since I last saw Kendall Hall, yet I understand it still exists. Though I am almost at the age when I might be a candidate for its ministrations, I have no desire to renew the acquaintance. It is not that the six months I spent working there were notably unpleasant, though they were strange. I remember that time vividly, but as if the events that occurred hadn't happened to me, but I had read them in a novel or acted in them in a play. When you are in a long run, you can often later recollect very clearly what you did and said, and what others said to you, on stage. You can recall what you felt too, even though those feelings were those of the character you played and not yours. That is how I remember Kendall Hall.

It had been built as a private sanatorium around 1900 and stood in its own quite extensive grounds. It was three storeys high and built of bricks the colour of dried blood. Along the ground floor façade ran a glass-covered veranda like a greenhouse through which you could see the desiccated blooms of elderly performers sitting and staring at the lawn and the plane trees beyond. To me, there was always something irreducibly grim about the place, even though some of the staff and inmates did their best to lighten the atmosphere.

My tasks were general: cleaning, working in the kitchen, making beds, wheeling tea trolleys and waiting at table. As most of the staff were female and, in those days, I was quite fit, I was summoned if any heavy lifting was required, or if any of the inmates had a fall, a not infrequent occurrence. My status as a "resting" professional actor counted in my favour, since I could, as Mr Dibdin, the Hall's Warden, put it, "relate to the old dears." This was true, to a certain extent, but many of the clientele of Kendall Hall belonged to the variety side of show business, as opposed to what those in variety called "legit", or actors like me. These "non legits", though they fascinated me, were, to some extent, alien beings.

Because I needed the money, I would often do nights at Kendall Hall, ready to help out if any untoward incident occurred. Very often nothing did, and I would sit through the night, in the staff room just off the entrance hall, bathed in silence, an oddly exhilarating experience.

Occasionally the inmates (as I will call them) put on a show in the evening. One would tell ancient gags, another would belt out songs ("Any Old Iron" for some reason being a favourite), and there was a reasonably good magic act. The legits occasionally took part by reciting slabs of Shakespeare, or performing little sketches, but these were barely tolerated by the variety side and with good reason. You could tell that there had been talent, but what talent there was on display, like a very old suit of good clothes, was now threadbare, moth-eaten and coming apart at the seams. These evening sessions were not exactly enjoyable, but they were interesting in a melancholy way, and it was at one of these events that I first really noticed Mrs Vandeleur.

"Old Mrs Vandeleur," she was called by the staff because she was in her nineties and probably the oldest inmate. She was sitting at the back in a wheelchair and staring vacantly at the stage where an ancient comic with hideously elastic features was executing a slow and rather flat-footed tap dance. I looked away, unable to take this macabre performance any longer, and studied the audience instead.

Mrs Vandeleur was very white and withered, but her eyes, though empty of expression, were vividly blue, like those of a new-born baby. Unlike most of the older inmates she was not slumped in her wheelchair, but sat upright, though I could tell it was costing her an effort to do so. I wondered whether she had once been beautiful and concluded that she must have been, though there was nothing in her features that could have told me. Age had not sharpened and clarified them, as it sometimes does, but rendered them indistinct and flabby. It was simply the way she held herself, with a distant, almost instinctive pride, that told me.

I noticed that her right knee was beginning to move up and down in time with the ponderous clacking of the performer's tap shoes. Otherwise there was not the least indication that she was paying attention to the act. Then her right leg kicked out, revealing from under her night gown a small and perfectly formed foot in a white stocking. This movement evidently hurt because I saw a spasm of pain cross her face as she withdrew her leg.

Thereafter she remained motionless until the end of the dance, when she made a little gesture to the nurse behind her. This was evidently the signal for her to be wheeled from the room.

Later that evening I asked that nurse, whose name was Curdella, about Mrs Vandeleur. Curdella was a large young woman, smiling but serious, an active member of a nearby Pentecostal church. She once invited me to attend a service there and, though curious, I declined the offer out of anticipated embarrassment. Might I be invited to confess my sins or speak in tongues?

"Oh, yes," said Curdella. "That Mrs Vandeleur, she's a strange one. You don't know what's going on inside her. She's very old. Someone told me she was a big star once, but that was long, long ago. She says she don't remember."

"What was her stage name?"

"Well her Christian name is Elsie, though she likes to be called Mrs Vandeleur. But someone once told me. Elsie... something. It was a lovely name, that I remember."

"Not Elsie Grace?" Quite unexpectedly and absurdly my heart was beating faster.

"Why yes! Grace! I knew it was a beautiful word. Like the Grace of God."

"Has she been here long?"

"Ever since I been here. But I believe she came from a private mental home. She'd been paid for by family, but when they didn't want to pay no longer and she was safe and quiet anyway, she came here. She don't talk much. It's like she's okay but she's not all there, if you know what I mean."

I could not get it out of my head that I had actually seen Elsie Grace, and that only a few months before I had bought four photographs of her from a collector's fair in Norwich. I knew that all of us have a tendency to forge a meaning out of mere coincidence, but that did not stop me from speculating. I took the four postcards out of the drawer and put them in my pocket to take to work.

It was nearly a week before I encountered Elsie Grace again. Usually, for meals, she came down to the dining hall and sat at a table alone to eat. This was not because she had insisted on solitude, but because she was so silent and unresponsive that the others found it depressing to be with her. She did not appear to scorn her fellow inmates; she just seemed barely conscious of their presence. That hackneyed phrase that Curdella had used about Elsie being "not all there" seemed to sum up her situation precisely.

On this particular day she was apparently not well enough (or willing?) to make it to the dining hall, so I was delegated to bring her her lunch in her room on the second floor. I found her sitting by the window and staring, with her customary vacancy, at the sunlit lawn below. She was, as usual, erect and did not appear to be in any physical distress.

The room was much like the others that I had seen, if perhaps a little larger. It was painted a dreary pale mushroom hue and there was only one picture on the wall, a faded, amateurish watercolour of some pansies in a vase, perhaps her own work. There were a few neglected-looking books on a shelf, but otherwise nothing to indicate a personality. Other rooms that I had been in were crowded with framed posters and memorabilia, and always several photographs or portraits of the inhabitants in the days of their glory. Elsie Grace had nothing.

"Hello, Elsie," I said. "I've brought your lunch."

"Mrs Vandeleur!" she said. The voice had the quiver of old age, but was clear, emphatic, surprisingly deep. I had used the name "Elsie" deliberately to provoke a response and had got it. While I arranged the lunch for her at a table by the window, I noticed that she was looking at me the whole time but without expression.

When I had finished, I said: "I beg your pardon, Mrs Vandeleur, but you are Elsie Grace, aren't you?" There was a long pause before she replied.

"I was... I think..."

Then I made the decisive step. I took out the four postcards that I was carrying with me and showed them to her. She studied each one minutely with a puzzled expression, laying them in a neat pile on the table beside her plate when she had finished her scrutiny.

"Where did you get these?"

I thought I detected a flicker of anger in her eyes. I explained their origin.

"So, you are on the stage?"

"Yes."

"You'll get nothing but misery out of it."

I began to protest mildly.

"Nothing but misery," she repeated. She

swept the postcards onto the floor and, as I bent to pick them up, she began to examine her lunch, but without any visible enthusiasm. Having picked the cards up I decided it was time to leave her to her meal, but she stopped me.

"Young man!" She pointed a long trembling finger at her bookcase. "The one with the torn...thing."

"Dust jacket?"

She nodded. "Mmm... Theatre..."

I saw the book she meant at once. It had a torn dust jacket, on which, over a colourful painted design of plum-coloured theatre curtains with gilded tassels and fringes, was inscribed the title: *Our Theatres of Yesteryear*. The author was someone called Clarence Vane-Partridge, a name with which I was vaguely familiar. I had seen it on books I had found in my grandmother's house, works of nostalgia, celebrating the late Victorian and Edwardian stage.

"Page 113," she said.

I opened it at the page indicated. Several paragraphs had been heavily underlined in blue pencil.

"Read it!" she said. I began to read. "Aloud!" she commanded. I obeyed.

"Following *A Midsummer Maid* in the spring of 1906 came another triumph with *The Peppermint Girl*, this time with music by Ivan Caryll and Lionel Monckton. The programme had all the good old names on it, but there was a new one. Well, stars had a habit of being born at the Gaiety, perhaps this new venture would see the birth of a new star as well. It did.

"The part of Miss Phoebe Sunbeam was taken by one Elsie Grace. And was anyone more aptly named? It may have been a comparatively small and inconsequential role, but Mr Monckton had written her a special number which brought the house down every night:

> *I'm a fairy sunbeam*
> *Flitting through the trees*
> *Tickling the daffodils*
> *Floating on the breeze.*

"Her voice was sweet, if small, but when she danced! It was not dancing; it was a piece of silvery thistledown floating in starlight. She did not touch the stage with her dainty feet, she was blown by the breeze, hither and thither. And then she kicked! Up went her leg, up went her little shoe, far above that golden head, without any visible effort, just as the wind might blow a spray of apple blossom or honeysuckle. And that kick knocked us all for six. Seldom has anyone so fresh danced so suddenly or so completely into the firmament of fame. In the space of a few days her face was to be everywhere, to gaze at us from magazines and from the innumerable picture postcards which we bought so eagerly to stick in our albums and send to our friends.

"All the stage-door Johnnies in London were at her delicate feet. Many were the baskets of flowers that ornamented her dressing room, some bedecked with precious gems and notes that read: 'I just wanted these roses to see you!'"

When I had finished reading, she said: "Words! Just words! I don't remember any of it!" The bitterness startled me. I wanted to pursue the conversation but she waved me away, pretending to concentrate on her lunch. When I came to collect it later, Elsie was asleep in her chair and the meal was barely touched.

After that I tried whenever possible to see and talk to her, but without much success. I don't think that she remembered me when I next saw her and when once I tried to address her as Elsie, she waved me away with that imperious gesture of hers. Thereafter she was always Mrs Vandeleur. I began to research her as far as I could. In the days before the internet, it was not easy. From an old *Who's Who in the Theatre* I gleaned the information that she had married a Thomas Vandeleur in 1913 ("no issue") and that thereafter her theatrical credits had dwindled, ceasing altogether in 1915; after which her life, according to the records, was a blank. The peak of her career would appear to have come with her debut in *The Peppermint Girl*, and, without exactly diminishing for several years following, not to have progressed. So many artistic careers have suffered the same trajectory, but hers seemed to me an extreme case.

One day when I was in a record shop which specialised in vintage discs and compilations of old recordings, I came across an LP entitled *Gaiety Glamour*. It had been made in the late sixties and consisted in a remastered selection of early recordings of numbers from Gaiety Theatre musicals. On the back of the sleeve there was a list of about twenty tracks. Here among them was Gertie Millar singing "I'm such a silly when the moon comes out...", and George Grossmith Jnr with *I say, Bertie, why do you bound?* – remembered now, if at all, because it features so memorably in Saki's "The Open Window". And here, yes, here, almost the last track, was: "'Fairy Sunbeam' (Lionel Monckton) from *The Peppermint Girl* (1906) Elsie Grace." I paid the exorbitant price that was demanded of me and left with the record.

As soon as I had got back to my flat. I put it on the record player. The tune, like the words, was slight to the point of silliness:

> *I'm a fairy sunbeam*
> *Flitting through the trees*
> *Tickling the daffodils*
> *Floating on the breeze...*

...but it was oddly memorable for all that. It evoked an era when trivial whimsy was not scorned or laughed at, but simply enjoyed. Once again I was conscious of that curious sense of nostalgia for a world I had never known: of audiences in evening dress, of champagne suppers at *Romano's,* of gaslit streets and "carriages at eleven."

Over the record's hiss and crackle, Elsie's voice was small and sharp, a little needle of sound that pricked that early recording's grunting accompaniment. (In the days before electronic microphones refined the quality of sound, recorded orchestras consisted mainly of the more easily audible brass and woodwind sections.) After she had sung a verse and a chorus or two, there was an orchestral interlude, during which, one presumes, the listener could imagine her legendary ethereal dancing. The plodding brass did little to evoke it, but I thought I could picture the scene even to the moment when the shriek of a piccolo announced her famous high kick.

I listened to the track several times until the tune was playing over and over in in my head whether I liked it or not, and I had no need of a recording. I wondered if I should take the record to play to Elsie. What would be her reaction? The idea was absurd. Who was I after all to do such a thing? A mere cleaner and handyman, an ex-actor: like Elsie now, I was a nothing.

A few days later I was on night watch. Curdella was with me in the staff room, a reassuring presence. While I read novels and biographies, she would study the Bible, earnestly highlighting passages in coloured markers, and consulting paper-backed commentaries. We would take it in turns to patrol the corridors, listening out for any disturbance or complaint from the inmates.

That night, at about 2 a.m., Curdella, who was more zealous in these activities than I, came into the staff room to announce that Mrs Vandeleur had had a fall and my assistance was required to return her to bed.

Elsie was lying on the floor in the middle of the room and appeared to be attempting to reach the door, though for what reason she could not say. She was making little inarticulate moaning sounds in which I could detect a word or phrase or two, the clearest of which appeared to be: "Where am I?"

Curdella was as strong as I was, and, as Elsie was almost uncannily light, we managed to return her to her bed without much difficulty or injury to ourselves. Elsie remained placid during this operation and did not cry out with pain, from which we inferred that no bones had been broken.

Elsie's was a standard geriatric bed, the sides of which should have been up to prevent her from straying, but this, for reasons unknown, had been neglected.

"I will have to report that," said Curdella, conscientious as always. There was a moan from the bed. "What is it, darling?"

"I'm alone," said Elsie. "Don't leave me."

"All right, Mrs Vandeleur," said Curdella. "I'll stay by you, till you get off to sleep." Then addressing me: "You go back down stairs now. I'll just sit here by the bed."

"Not you! Him!" said Elsie, waving a finger in my direction. Curdella looked surprised and offended.

"You want *him* to sit with you, do you, darling?"

"Of course! And don't call me 'darling'! You may go." Elsie's voice was emphatic.

"All right, all right, Mrs Vandeleur. I go." She turned to me. "You okay with that?"

"Fine."

"You ring if you need me. I'll be down there, praying for her."

I nodded. She left the room, still hurt by the dismissal. When she had gone, Elsie said: "Will you hold my hand, young man?" I took it. It was smooth and cold, like a piece of polished marble; the grip was surprisingly firm.

For a long time nothing was to be heard in the room except her breathing. I thought she would soon be asleep, but her grip did not relax. Curdella had left a dim light on in the room, and I could see that Elsie was lying flat on her back, eyes open, staring at the ceiling.

"Where am I?" she asked eventually.

"Kendall Hall."

"What is that?"

"It's your home."

"No. I have no home. Who am I?"

"Mrs Vandeleur."

"Yes. Yes. But who am I?"

"You're Elsie Grace."

"Am I? Why?"

There could be no answer; I was silent.

"Why? How?"

There was desperation in her voice. Clearly she was not simply going to fall asleep. Very gently I began to hum the tune of "Fairy Sunbeam". When I stopped, she told me urgently to go on. This time I began to sing the words of the chorus:

I'm a fairy sunbeam
Flitting through the trees
Tickling the daffodils
Floating on the breeze...

And when I faltered, she completed it in the faintest possible voice, but in time and in tune:

Leaping over lily pads,
Sporting in the sun,
Dancing on the dandelions:
Oh, what fun!

And with the final words, her right leg gave a little twitch like a reflex action. Was this a ghost of the famous kick?

"You remember?" I said.

"Idiotic! 'Oh, what fun!' Not fun at all."

I tried to release my hand from hers, but she gripped it even more tightly.

"No. Hold on. I think I'm... Close your eyes." I obeyed. "Tell, me."

Tell her what? Then, though my eyes were closed, I saw. I was standing in almost complete darkness, but looking down I could see a pair of small feet beneath a long white nightdress of the kind that Elsie was wearing. Looking up I found myself gazing into a long dark distance which, though almost without light, seemed to possess dimension; but whether that dimension was of space or time, I could not tell. These speculations passed through my head, but had little effect on my mind, which was concentrated wholly on the experience. In the far distance, as if at the end of an immense corridor or tunnel, was a patch of light in which there was a confusion of movement and sound.

"Tell me," she said.

I tried to describe what I was seeing.

"There's too much dark between. Make it come closer."

She gripped my hand tighter and I concentrated. Whether I was moving closer to it, or it was coming towards me, I cannot say, but it did, though it was still diffuse. There were sounds randomly gathered, like an orchestra tuning up, and the images similarly were fragmentary and superimposed. But it was a world with a distinctive tone and feel: perhaps not so much one orchestra tuning up, but several orchestras all playing different pieces of music by the same composer. I was beginning to distinguish some of the fragments: here was a row of footlights, then a chasm, then a row of white shirt fronts and bejewelled evening dresses. Almost as soon as these impressions became distinct, they started to fade while, simultaneously, Elsie's grip on my hand relaxed until it fell away altogether. I heard the faint sound of snoring and opened my eyes. Elsie was asleep. I laid her hand over her chest, tucked her in and left the room.

The following morning, Elsie was too weak to get out of bed. Curdella said that she would report it to the Warden of Kendall Hall and suggest that her next of kin be sent for.

"I think she is on the way out," she said.

"Has she got a next of kin?"

"There is a great niece. She visited once, not for long. Nearly a year ago now. That's all I know." She sighed. "I just pray Mrs Vandeleur can accept Jesus as her Saviour before the end."

"How do you know she hasn't already accepted him?"

"Oh, no, not yet! I can tell. Oh, no!" She shook her head gravely, as if speaking out of a deep well of spiritual experience.

Mr Dibdin, the Warden, an amiable but rather lazy man, evidently heeded Curdella's advice because a couple of days later a sage green Range Rover drew up on the gravel drive outside Kendall Hall. From it stepped the kind of woman you might expect to emerge from a sage green Range Rover: in her thirties, puffa jacket, tweed skirt and pearls adorning the neck of a dove grey polo-necked jumper. Over her blonde hair was tied a colourful silk headscarf on which horseshoes had been printed in profusion. There were no black Labradors in the back of her car, but I guessed there might have been, had she been nearer to home than Croydon. Despite appearing to conform to a type, she was not unattractive, and she announced herself as Trish Hope-Duckenfield.

"I'm the great niece," she said, by way of further explanation.

She had a brisk way of talking which suggested that her visit was one of duty rather than sentiment. I was selected to show her up to Elsie's room.

As we were going upstairs, she said: "I gather from old Dibdin that Great Auntie Elsie is on her last legs."

"We believe so."

"Ah, well. About time she popped the clogs. You new here?"

"Sort of."

"Well, glad you're doing the honours. Last time I was escorted by some Jamaican woman. Not that I've got anything against them, but she would keep banging on about Jesus. Had a funny name too. Cruella, or something like that."

"Curdella?"

"That's it! I was mixing her up with *101 Dalmatians*. Loved that book as a kid. Is she still here?"

"Very much so." I brought her to a stop in front of Elsie's room.

"Well, I think I may give her a miss, this time round, if you don't mind. This Elsie?" I nodded. "Here we go! Family duty!" she said, then knocked and went in.

When she emerged about twenty minutes later, she was more subdued. "Yes, definitely on the downward slope, I'd say. You were right to call me. Mind you, she didn't have much of a clue who I was. Thought I was her mother at one point, but that's par for the course. Still, she's had a good innings... Well, a long one, at any rate. Poor old Auntie Elsie." She seemed on the verge of being upset, so I invited her down for a cup of tea in the staff room.

There she explained to me her connection with Elsie. She was no blood relation, being a Vandeleur by birth and the granddaughter of the brother of Tom Vandeleur who had married Elsie.

"We don't know much about her," she said, "except for ages we had to pay for her to be put up in an expensive private loony bin until she was moved here. I gather the marriage to Great Uncle Tom was not a huge success, to say the least. Can't entirely blame her. Great Uncle Tom was a bit of an S H one T, by all accounts. Never liked him myself. Even as a kid you knew not to go too near him, if you get my drift. Well, Auntie Elsie took to the bottle and went Doolally, and Great Uncle Tom couldn't cope, so he bunged her in this private bin, and, when he died, we found he had got through almost all his money, though he had had pots of the stuff. So, the rest of the family had to fork out for Auntie Elsie's keep which, as you can imagine, didn't endear. Added to which, I gather, she hadn't been exactly out of the top drawer. Something of a gold digger, I should imagine. Wasn't she on the stage, or something? Hence Kendall Hall."

"As a matter of fact, she was quite a big star at one time."

"Good God! Really? What was she in?"

"Musicals. Or Musical Comedy, as it was then called."

"Musicals, eh? Well, that's not really our sort of thing. Don't really hold with that *Jesus Christ Superstar* nonsense and all those stupid American doo-dahs. No time for it. Mind you I did once go to *Salad Days*. Now that was quite jolly. My husband had been at Eton with Julian Slade, you see. Do you know *Salad Days?*"

I said I was familiar with it.

"Now that, I admit, was rather jolly. You seem to know a bit about this sort of thing. Was that the kind of musical Great Auntie Elsie was in?"

"I suppose... In a way." How strange it would have seemed to me then had I been informed that within a few months of this first encounter I was to have a brief and passionate affair with Trish Hope-Duckenfield. Yet such improbabilities, after all, are what make life bearable. Even then, I had some respect for her sense of duty, if for little else.

When I shook hands with her beside the Range Rover that was to take her home to Hampshire, Trish was back to her normal brusque self: "You'll let me know when she finally pegs out, won't you?" I said I would.

I was to learn that people who are dying often hang on for longer than you expect. That was the case with Elsie. She remained in her room and I would take her up her meals. Curdella had told Dibdin that I had established some rapport with her and, though there may have been some truth in this, there were days when Elsie barely acknowledged me. Her unclouded blue eyes were focussed on distant objects far beyond the confines of her room. There was a look of search about her, but it was troubled and restless.

I had made a recording of *Gaiety Glamour* onto cassette tape and one day I brought it in to play for her. It was four in the afternoon and she was sitting up in bed listlessly sipping a cup of tea when I switched on the player. She paid scant attention to Gertie Millar, George Grossmith and the others, but when I turned over the tape and played her song, she was instantly alert. When it was over, she said "Again!" and gripped my hand. I wound back the tape and played it once more. Her grip became tighter; instinctively I closed my eyes.

The stage was a dazzle of lights. The scenery was a woodland glade, delicately painted, like something out of Claude or Poussin, and across the footlights beyond the orchestra pit, the faint gleam of white shirt front and jewelled silk. I felt myself carried across the stage by the sweep of the strings in the orchestra, and something more intangible. It was as if the audience itself were lifting me by an act of collective will. I looked up to see a man in evening dress enter the prompt side stage box. He wore a top hat and a cape, and his eyes were on me, even as he closed the door of the box. Turning from it, still standing, he removed his hat and cape, and began to take off a pair of white kid gloves. All the while he was staring at me. Carefully he laid the gloves on the red velvet lip of the box and sat down, still fixed on me. He was dark and though not exactly handsome was imposing. He had a heavy black moustache and the lips beneath it were dark red. I felt myself held by his gaze, but still I floated, not dropping a step or a note. A quick glance behind me and I saw that the chorus too, even as they danced, had noticed the man in the box and his eyes on me. A smile of conspiracy passed between them and me. I looked up at him and saw a flash of anger in his eyes.

"...Oh, what fun!"

There was a burst of applause, even a few cheers. He took the white rose from his buttonhole and threw it at my feet. I picked it up, put it to my lips, looked at him. There was a renewed surge of applause. I bowed and ran with light feet off stage.

There was a confusion of light and noise and I was coming out of the stage door. Boys, and some girls too, handed me little bunches of violets. I signed the postcards. At some distance he stood, under a streetlamp so he would be noticed. The cloak, the hat, a gold topped cane, the white kid gloves. He made no sign, just looked with his great solemn dark eyes, as if he knew I would come to him. Then flowers, jewels; a table in a crowded restaurant; a ring with a diamond in it; champagne in a silvery bucket sweating with the cold; a cold church too, but full of light and orange blossoms. I was lying in a strange bed in a strange room. The man entered in a brocaded dressing gown; he closed the door, his eyes fixed on me. He paused, then turned and locked the door before advancing towards me. For a moment I felt his breath...

Elsie's grip relaxed. I heard her murmur something. I became aware of being myself again, but still I saw things, now vague and shadowy. I saw a door closing; I heard it slam shut and a key turning in the lock. Elsie's hand fell from mine. The dream, or whatever it was, faded. She was asleep. Some tea had spilled and I cleaned it up.

Later that day I played Elsie's song on the cassette recorder to Curdella. She listened to it gravely. I told her that it brought back memories for Elsie.

"Maybe," said Curdella, "but it is not a good song. There are no fairies, but there are devils. This is a devil song. Perhaps I will play her some of my gospel choir tapes. They are good songs."

I understand she did play them, but they were not well received.

I would often visit Elsie, even when there was no necessity, and always I would bring my cassette player because she demanded it. I had recorded the song so that it would play repeatedly. While I played it she would stretch out her hand to be held.

I saw things that perhaps I shouldn't have. I saw fragments of a life, not always in the order of their time. The dark man was always there with his great dark eyes, the stare either enraged, or full of the dead cold look of possession. The world began to spin around me. Sometimes Elsie would cry out and I let go of her hand but she would insist, I held her hand again. The scene darkened. It moved from the bedroom to the hall of a house: black and white flagstones like a chess board, a hat stand made from the antlers of a stag. Every time I advanced towards it, he would be there, turning the key in the lock. Then there were other hallways and corridors, colder, brighter, more clinical, but always doors shutting and keys turning in locks.

After these events she would be calmer, but she would often ask me to leave her with the cassette player. I left it with her permanently, and I gave her the postcards too when she requested them.

Then there was one night. It was close and a thunderstorm brooded. I was in the staff room with Curdella on night duty. I noticed that she was frowning with concentration as she read her Bible, a sure sign that her attention was insecure. I had abandoned my book and was allowing myself to submit to the restlessness of the moment. When I glanced at Curdella, she became aware and looked up with an irritated expression.

"You know, *you* should be studying the Word," she said.

I recognised this as the preliminary to one of those occasional theological discussions we had begun to have. They were never very fierce, even if they did not seem to me to achieve much, except to help pass the time. A faint flash was visible beyond the curtains, and a few seconds later we heard the murmur of thunder. Then came the hiss of rain. I felt a cold breeze from somewhere.

"Oh, Lord, what is going on?" said Curdella. I shrugged, determined not to submit to the unease we obviously both felt. All was quiet within.

Suddenly it was not. The door of the staff room blew open with a bang.

"Someone must have left a window open downstairs," I said. It was a perfectly plausible explanation, but I was not convinced by it. We ran out into the hall where the front door stood open, flapping on its hinges. Beyond the door the falling rain became momentarily a bright screen of silver beads as another flash of lightening came and went with thunder at its heels.

We shut the door and bolted it.

"It should never have been left open," I said.

"It wasn't left open," said Curdella. "Get real!"

Then the banging began. It came from upstairs, as if all the doors of all the rooms were opening and closing. We ran upstairs and began closing the doors, reassuring agitated inmates as we did so. On the second floor we saw something white lying in the corridor like a crumpled sheet.

She lay face down in her nightgown in the passage beyond the open door of her room. We turned her over. It was Elsie. Inside the room the cassette player was singing the Fairy Sunbeam song.

"Turn that off!" said Curdella. I waited till the number had ended with the curious shriek of the piccolo and its heavy final chord, then I went into Elsie's room and switched off the machine.

When I returned Curdella was cradling Elsie's body in her arms.

"She's gone." As we stared at the calm, sleeping face, Curdella said: "My lord! Now you can tell she was beautiful."

I attended the brief service at Croydon Crematorium on behalf of Kendall Hall, and the only other person present was Trish Hope-Duckenfield. Curdella had wanted to come, but illness prevented her. It was a desolate event, as these things are when the subject is unknown to the officiating clergyman, and barely known to those attending. It began at noon and was over by half past twelve. I felt something more needed to be done to mark Elsie's passing so, on an impulse, I invited Trish to have lunch with me at a small Italian restaurant in Croydon. At least we could drink a glass of Chianti to her memory, but when we got there Trish ordered champagne. And so began a brief, unregretted episode in my life which I remember now as if it had been a play and I a mere performer in it. Perhaps on my deathbed, like Elsie, I will reconnect. Who knows?

A few weeks later I auditioned for a part in a Pinero play at Chichester and got it. My understanding of the Edwardian idiom was particularly appreciated by the director, so I took my leave of Kendall Hall. Curdella, by this time a friend, gave me as a leaving present a copy of a book called *Path to Salvation* which I still have somewhere, unread of course; I gave her my record of *Gaiety Glamour* and the postcard of Elsie Grace in *The Peppermint Girl*.

In life Elsie had become a ghost, now she was one no longer. Once more she was the fairy sunbeam, to me and perhaps Curdella, if to no-one else. She did not even merit a mention in the obituary columns, but she was past caring. As I made my way down the drive, away from Kendall Hall for the last time, the sun was glinting through the green branches, and that idiotic little tune was repeatedly skipping through my brain:

> *I'm a fairy sunbeam*
> *Flitting through the trees*
> *Tickling the daffodils*
> *Floating on the breeze.*
> *Leaping over lily pads,*
> *Sporting in the sun,*
> *Dancing on the dandelions:*
> *Oh, what fun!*

Its hold on my mind was damned irritating, but a small price to pay for her release.

Holidays from Hell (Tartarus Press, 2017)
The Ballet of Dr Caligari and Madder Mysteries
(Tartarus Press, 2019)

Collected and Selected Editions
Dramas from the Depths (Centipede Press, 2010)
Shadow Plays (Egaeus 2012)
The Sea of Blood (Dark Regions Press, 2016)

For Children
*The Hauntings at Tankerton Park and How They
Got Rid of Them* (Zagava 2016)

Novels
Virtue in Danger (Zagava 2013)
The Dracula Papers (Chômu Press, 2011)
The Boke of the Divill (Dark Regions Press, 2018)

Now available and forthcoming from
Black Shuck Shadows:

Shadows 1 – The Spirits of Christmas
by Paul Kane

Shadows 2 – Tales of New Mexico
by Joseph D'Lacey

Shadows 3 – Unquiet Waters
by Thana Niveau

Shadows 4 – The Life Cycle
by Paul Kane

Shadows 5 – The Death of Boys
by Gary Fry

Shadows 6 – Broken on the Inside
by Phil Sloman

Shadows 7 – The Martledge Variations
by Simon Kurt Unsworth

Shadows 8 – Singing Back the Dark
by Simon Bestwick

blackshuckbooks.co.uk/shadows